The Tale Of Miss Berta London

"Recollections of Accomplishments"

JIHAN LATIMER

DEDICATION

Miss Berta struggles through a series of complicated situations and metamorphoses from a self-interested fashion editor to a well-respected humanitarian for the youth. Miss Berta's adventures in this tale encourage positive ideals for the young generation, which foster a sense of conviction. Positive stories encourage us to achieve the impossible. Good books breed good minds, regardless of circumstances. This book is dedicated to today's youth, because the future lies in the hands of the younger generation.

PROLOGUE

Miss Berta's professional career as the fashion editor for *Eloquent Fashion Magazine* was beyond her expectations. Her mother was a well-respected fashion icon, so it was deemed that Miss Berta would follow in her mother's footsteps, to dominate the world of fashion. Her fall from grace teaches Miss Berta that life is more than the superficial world around her. Hitting rock bottom, Miss Berta has no choice but to become a nanny for a wealthy family. Miss Berta finds herself having to adapt to a new social status, which at first proves difficult but eventually leads her to become more grounded. She soon discovers a way to combine her publishing know-how with her new values, to create a family magazine that helps bring families closer together. Being exposed to a new world outside of the fashion industry, Miss Berta evolves into a humanitarian.

CONTENTS

1

WHO IS MISS BERTA?

A strange woman with a mean grin paraded through the hustle-bustle streets of New York City. The cars were obnoxiously loud, beeping their horns, shuffling past one another in the chaos. People were scattered from the north, south, east, and west of the city, trying to find taxis, catch the underground rail train, or find the nearest bus stop.

Living downtown was the norm for Miss Berta London. She commuted back and forth from her home to her job, and lived only fifteen blocks away from work in the well-known, popular Eloquent Headquarters located on East Sixty-Eighth Street. The Upper East Side was the sophisticated side of New York City. The rich and wealthy belonged on this side of town. Living and working in this big, saturated, expensive city, Miss Berta watched the ill-dressed individuals. She walked past them with frustration on her way to work. The onlookers, on the contrary, watched her with amazement and envy because of her extravagant style of dress.

Miss Berta always set the fashion trends for the start of each season. Her eyeglasses were of the vintage style of the 1950s era. Her long, draped dress covered her entire lower body. She had on brown flat shoes, to complement her feet. She wore brown shoes everywhere, with her strange mahogany-colored beret hat and blazer, along with her button-up blouses. Her short, shoulder-length hair was ebony black and cut in an orderly coif. The young generation of New Yorkers imitated this hairstyle. Miss Berta was a genius among them; they admired her daring attitude of ostentation. In her mind, fashion was art. It was colorful, dull, bright, or polka dot stripes—anything the trends needed to be for that specific era. As the seasons changed, so, too, would Miss Berta's fashion trends. New York City propelled her creativity; it was responsible for her fashion genius, and influenced her fashion sense. Women from history also influenced her: Marie Antoinette and Queen Victoria. Both were queens of their respective lands who transcended the fashion era of their époque. In the weekly newspaper articles, some media critics compared her to Queen Victoria, with a modern twist. Other critics espoused her as Marie Antoinette, the experimental fashion icon, because she always knew what was hip, although she herself never gave into the trends from other competitors.

A brightly lit building with a eye catching red, black, and yellow billboard displayed the words *Eloquent Fashion Magazine: Elitism Is Our Motto.* The billboard promoted the fall season fashion line with a slideshow of models wearing purplish-blue ostrich-style dresses. These were elongated dresses, accessorized by feathers.

Not only was this building reflecting the creative artistic capabilities Miss Berta possessed, it was also Miss Berta's sanctuary. The entire building was an extension of her outer self. The building epitomized fashion. Fashion was her escape from reality and the invention of who she was as a person.

On Miss Berta's daily walk toward the vibrant *Eloquent Fashion Magazine* building, she noticed the advertisements that surrounded the building. These advertisements were placed in front of independent clothing stores. Managers and directors of these businesses alike felt if they were to be located near this grand building, they, too, had a promising future in the world of fashion. These independent stores fueled Miss Berta's competitiveness. She constantly had to think outside the box from her competitors. It was a challenge because these local, independent clothing stores imitated everything she did. In a way, they were spies, who wanted to know what the secret was to her constant success.

As Miss Berta continually walked past the degraded New York City subway system, she noticed graffiti on the walls of the train station, which led to the escalators toward the exit. The spray-painted graffiti on the walls of the subway gave her an idea that would change her career in fashion forever.

Graffiti would be one of the new themes for the future, but not for the upcoming photo shoot, which would promote the fall issue of the magazine and feature nature and vintage elements. The autumn leaves fell and were brown, and Miss Berta decided this was the direction she wanted for the magazine's upcoming release.

Nevertheless, she did take photographs of the graffiti-covered buildings. There was a particular design she noticed on the ally building she had passed. It was a large rose on the side of the brick building, which was spray-painted in bright neon colors. The image took her breath away. She took a snapshot of the image and sent it with a text, which read, "Something to consider working with in the future." Romero, one of her trusted colleagues received the message in a matter of seconds.

On her way to work, she passed Logan High School, a prestigious, co-educational school. The inner-city schoolchildren approached Miss Berta and asked for her autograph, but she snarled them away. Many middle school and high school children were constantly late each morning, because they wanted to witness Miss Berta's daily passing as she entered the glamorous *Eloquent Fashion Magazine* building, which was guarded by an intense amount of security.

"Stay back!" Miss Berta's main security guard, Xenox, a muscular man scowled, blocking the children from Miss Berta's passage, as she shoved past the crowd. They constantly took photographs of her, while sticking out their pens and notebooks for her to autograph their issue of *Eloquent Fashion Magazine*.

"Please! Sign this for me?" one girl cried, but Miss Berta was indifferent to her request.

"Miss Berta!" The crowd yelled. Some attempted to grab her clothing, but others were more restrained because they were too frightened of her security. Miss Berta relied on Xenox for everything. He was her head security. His responsibilities exceeded the other two security guards'. Miss Berta had high regard for him, because she relied on him to keep her safe at all times. Lex, Miss Berta's second line of security, was relaxed, kind, and friendly. Miss Berta usually relied on Lex for emotional support. He always had a positive quote or word to bestow on Miss Berta in times of need. Moe was her third line of defense. He was nonchalant and sluggish. He was on board because Miss Berta needed a third security guard, due to the shoving crowds, which fought to get near her. One late afternoon, Miss Berta could not walk down the street without being harassed by a crowd of people. It took her security guards a few hours to get her through the crowd that day, as night descended. Nevertheless, they managed the task and were successful, and Miss Berta was finally home.

Miss Berta lived in a luxuriously strange house with mahogany-brown curtains and two eighteenth century–style pianos—one in her living room and the other in her recreation room; a room Miss Berta kept for sketching and painting. Both pianos were white as snow and were freshly new, though they gave off a musty scent. The navy-blue king-size couches took up a big portion of the living room space. The living room had a hallway, which led to a circular hall used for dancing. (This space never got utilized; it was merely a passageway into the kitchen.) The living room floor was made of marble material. The chandeliers were exquisitely decorated in Art Deco style and lit the high ceiling brightly.

Miss Berta's chef, Cephas Pasteur, was French; he made all her meals. He found his home in Miss Berta's kitchen. Miss Berta also had two housekeepers: Christine, a short woman with a chubby, round face, whose responsibilities included washing and ironing Miss Berta's clothes, organizing her closet space, and walking her two dogs, who despised Alexis, the other housekeeper. The dogs attempted to attack him whenever he tried to take them out on their daily walks. His responsibilities were to vacuum all the carpeted floors, clean the bathrooms, scrub the bathtubs, and mop the floors to all five bedrooms in the house. Miss Berta never complained about her home and its upkeep because it was always immaculate.

Her neighbors spied on her frequently, peeking through their curtains. Mary Whitmore had been married to her husband Ralph, for twenty years. They both were sixty-five. Ralph was a very nonchalant man. His wife, on the contrary, was a nosy, nagging woman, who always wanted to know what was going on behind Miss Berta's closed doors. During weeknights and on Saturday, Mary Whitmore spent most of her time spying on Miss Berta. She sometimes invited Miss Berta to rendezvous with the neighbors.

Miss Berta frequently looked out her window to find Mary peering right back. "Any plans this Saturday Miss Berta?" and "How are your bulldogs,

Molly and Sarah?" Miss Whitmore yelled through the window of her upscale Manhattan condominium home one chilly, sunny morning.

"My business is my business, Whitmore!" Miss Berta announced in a disconcerting, cold, slithering tone.

"Not to worry," Mrs. Whitmore proclaimed, as she closed the curtains to her second-floor bedroom. Miss Berta watched her with an evil facial expression from her garden. Ralph had been observing the whole scene from his rocking chair near the window on the second floor, while Mrs. Whitmore gazed at him distastefully.

"She was right for that one dear," Mr. Whitmore proclaimed at his wife. Mrs. Whitmore was shocked at his response. She turned away. Ralph returned to watching the news. A middle-aged woman with brown hair on the television screen was corresponding with her news-anchor counterpart. Both were dressed in suits, discussing the stagnant economy of 2008. Miss Berta was thirty-nine years old, facing a middle-age crisis. She had so much responsibility as editor in chief of *Eloquent Fashion Magazine*, the top fashion magazine nationwide. She was in charge of making official decisions. The stylists picked out the wardrobe for the models, but Miss Berta had final approval over the wardrobe selections for the photo shoots. She also had recruiters, who were responsible for interviewing potential employees, but Miss Berta made the final hiring decisions. Her hired models were held to a high caliber and had to complete eight photographic shots in a period of three days. Her photographers were not like the usual photographers who gave detailed directions for every shot. The models had to adapt to every situation. Every day the set changed, the lighting changed, the stylists changed, hair and makeup designers changed their application and products. She held her staff highly responsible for their professionalism and attained skills.

Miss Berta was not a lethargic manager—one who relied on an assistant for help during the creative process for the magazine. Instead, she relied on herself. Her diligence drove people to be petrified of her. She had a heavy case of obsessive-compulsive disorder, especially on the job. She worked late night hours. The monstrosity of each late night at the office left her in anguish.

It was a typical Monday. Miss Berta paced the corridor of her dimly lit office. She searched and searched through the expired *Eloquent Fashion*

Magazine titles, which dated back to 1998. She browsed the pictures from the file cabinet of her assistant secretary Anna. Anna kept a record of *Eloquent Fashion Magazine*'s history. Each magazine, along with the magazine's yearly calendar, was filed chronologically. Miss Berta browsed through the year 2000's pictures. One faded picture took Miss Berta's fancy; it was one she had to enlarge at her home office studio. The year of the photo dated 1998.

The night was young. It was six o'clock when the sun began to fall. Miss Berta was in her multicolored sweater with the initials *EFM* in black on the back. She looked at a faded and tattered photograph, which lay on her desk. It caught her attention because her mother was in the picture. The photograph displayed in numbers the year 1998, the year her mother had died. The portrait of her mother was natural. It was the only photograph she had of her mother, without makeup and wearing simple clothing. Her mother looked to be fifty-eight. She looked so youthful and her clothes were conservative. The vintage-style piano in the picture gave Miss Berta the incentive to have nature and vintage elements in the magazine's upcoming release. Miss Berta dove into a brainstorming session for the magazine, grasping ideas from the photographs, which lay on her desk. She read a quote on a second photograph, which lay on her desk. It said: "Use nature tones." This was signed in her mother's writing. In the photo, her mother was twenty-five. Although the photograph was tattered, the nature-toned hat her mother wore gave her an idea. She jotted down notes about this natured toned greenish, brown hat her mother wore.

Miss Berta concluded that she should bring back natural vintage, bohemian style to her magazine. She clipped the picture to her overhead drawing board as a reminder. It was getting late at the office, so she grabbed her trench coat from where it hung, picked up her handbag, and placed her bright red beret hat on her head. As she exited the *EFM* building with her three-line of security guards, she found her driver outside waiting for her. Her line of security made sure they followed behind her driver, as he drove Miss Berta home.

She gathered her things from the car and exited without saying good-bye to her designated driver Luke, who was always silent on the drive home. Meanwhile, three of her security guards smiled and waved at her and drove off.

At home, Miss Berta turned off the living room light switch and yawned, then headed upstairs to her bedroom. In her brightly lit bathroom, she quickly washed her face and brushed her teeth and threw on her pajamas. The entire night caused her to fret over the layout and design for the magazine cover. In the world of Miss Berta London, life was simple, yet complex. Her philosophy was simple: "You're fired" or "Better get that fixed, and if it's not, you're fired." These two were her most popular phrases to use among her employees. She used them to keep her employees from neglecting their deadlines. She was very strict about time. All assignments had to be completed according to schedule.

The following day, employees at *Eloquent Fashion* Magazine were frantic due to preparations. The day of the photo-shoot was approaching and time was running out. Alfonzo Romero, an Italian photographer, was Miss Berta's loyal companion and photographer for *Eloquent Fashion Magazine*. Born and raised a perfectionist, his strategy as a photographer was very analytical. His process was slow and long. This strategy frustrated Heather, a model for *Eloquent Fashion Magazine*. She was constantly tired, especially of the constant criticism she received on a daily basis. It was a typical day at the headquarters and the stylists, photographers, and set designers moved about the building in a hastened pace. Romero stood in place with his multitudes of cameras surrounding him. He pointed toward a youngish-looking model named Heather Tilling, the magazine's top model.

"Turn your head sideways, turn your face to the right. Don't forget to attract the camera with your eyes." Romero rotated the camera around the set as he snapped photos. "Heather, I need you to smile," Romero announced. Heather followed his instruction cooperatively, but sulked as she felt the displeasure at being used as a live mannequin. Nevertheless, her hand movements were seamless and delicate. She shot eight camera shots with Romero. Romero repositioned three cameras, which were placed in a pyramid setup before him. The lighting crew worked around Romero. They contrasted the lighting on the set from a somber seamless backdrop to a green screen used for light reflection. Strobe lights were used. These lights were responsible for balancing daylight along with the studio light, to create a warmer lighting effect for the models. The hair and makeup team coordinated with the lighting crew and photographers. The lighting Romero set up, stripped the set from the nature toned theme Miss Berta anticipated.

Romero never spoke ill of his boss. Many nights during the winter season, Miss Berta kept him overnight. Romero illuminated the pictures he had taken of models earlier in the day to Photoshop them the next night.

"Romero, I want you to finish editing these photographs and have all of them completed to show me tomorrow." Romero humbly acknowledged her requests. "Sure thing. It's going to be an overnight job."

"What job isn't at *EFM*? Here, we are dedicated to being the best." Miss Berta closed the door behind her, as she left Romero to complete his Photoshop and Illustrator adaptations for the following morning.

It was 6:00 a.m. Monday morning. Miss Berta sat by her window, drinking blackberry tea. She looked into her garden, which flourished with white daisies, while observing her two bulldogs. As she watched the two dogs play with each other, she began to close her eyes slightly. Her mind took her back to when she was a little girl. Her father sat at the breakfast table, reading his newspaper and smoking a cigar.

"Daddy, do you have to go to work today?" Little Berta asked sadly. Her father wore his usual blue suit. "Yes dear, daddy's got to go to work to make you happy," he announced in his deep, stern voice. His response made her face fill with sadness, but she was aware that this was a typical day in her life. Each time, her parents left her at home with a nanny. She couldn't understand at that age why she spent most of her days with a person other than her parents. She wanted to be with them always. Little Berta was seven and a half. She was clinging to her teddy bear, as she watched her father intently read his daily newspaper and sip on a cup of coffee. "Well Scott and I will miss you daddy." She responded to her father. Mr. London smiled and lifted his daughter to place her onto his lap.

"Thomas, we have to get going!" A high-pitched voice from the corridor belted in agitation. A woman came strolling into the kitchen wearing bright red lipstick. She had shiny hair, which was cut into a short bob. She wore a mink coat and six-inch black leather heels. Mr. London and little Berta took their attention away from each other and focused on the vibrant woman who stood in front of them. Mr. London stood up and hugged her, as she entered the room.

Berta's mother laughed continuously at his advances. "Not now honey," replied the woman as she pushed Mr. London away.

"You promised Berta and me that all of us would be going camping instead of making an appearance for that photo shoot for the women of New York City, to express themselves as superior to everyone in the fashion world. It's not fair to Berta or me. We love you, they don't." Mr. London boldly announced.

Smugly, the woman crossed her arms in agitation. "Berta does not enjoy the outdoors, nor do I!" Mr. London said. "She is a shopaholic, like her mother." Mrs. London stated.

"Mommy!" Little Berta yelled loudly. The lady had her arms out to embrace little Berta, who ran toward her mother.

"Oh honey, I miss you already. We'll go shopping later," said Adline. Little Berta crossed her arms and pouted.

"I hate shopping, Mommy! I want to help children." She said.

Adline was shocked at this response. "Why honey?" Adline looked disappointed.

"Mommy, I want to help children, so they can be happy like me." Little Berta replied confidently.

Mr. London smiled at his daughter's words and sat down, while he continued to read his newspaper. "I don't think she's going for that today, Adline dearest," Mr. London answered, as his wife Adline rolled her eyes.

"Daddy doesn't understand the world of princesses, does he Berta?" Adline whispered to little Berta, who giggled to herself. Adline carried little Berta to the breakfast table, and placed her on her lap. Meanwhile, her daughter grabbed a piece of rye toast, and reached for the strawberry jam. She began to fiddle with the jar. As she twisted it sideways, she lost control of it.

"Careful Berta, Mommy's wearing Versace today!"

Little Berta simply looked up at her mother as the jam spilled all over her mother's expensive white suit. Berta trembled, as her legs were shaking, while she had her thumb in her mouth.

"Berta!" Adline screamed angrily at her little Berta.

Miss Berta opened her eyes and looked at her watch. She was back in her present reality. She was in her bedroom. The flowered linen curtains hanging above, draped over the window seal. Miss Berta lifted her head, as her ruffled hair fell to her shoulders. She looked around the room and saw her two dogs on the floor play fighting. "Quiet," Miss Berta ordered her two dogs. The dogs fell quiet. They had anticipated Miss Berta would throw a toy ball for them to chase after. "Oh darn, I'm late," she whispered to herself as she checked the time on her glamorous watch.

It was the day of a major event for the magazine. Miss Berta was no longer the innocent little girl in her flashback, who asked her father a million questions at a time, but a mature, stern and strict adult who had to prepare her team for an intense photo shoot for the fall issue.

At work that day, Miss Berta paced the hallways with frustration and anxiety because her daily tasks had fallen behind schedule. Romero had the layout of the entire show, ready to show Miss Berta. The entire staff was on crunch time, because the entire photo shoot had to be ready by tomorrow.

Top representatives from some of the best fashion companies were to attend. She relied on this shoot for them to recognize her vision. Representatives from *Belle*, *Aurora*, *Moi*, and *Chantel* designers came from all over the world in hopes that they were to be featured in *Eloquent Fashion Magazine*, to showcase their clothing to the world. Romero and Heather had the photographs Romero had taken the previous night. They awaited Miss Berta to give her approval of which designers would be showcased. These companies were well known in France, Monaco, Italy, South Africa, and Germany. The pressure was intense. Miss Berta's assistants scrambled around the room, trying to make sure the models were on cue, and the set designs were creatively assembled.

The models practiced their poses and runway walks. Everyone seemed to be aiming for perfection. "*C'est aujourd'hui*, let's look alive, people! Heather, you look terrible!"

"I'm sorry Berta, I thought—" stated Heather, her arms crossed. Miss Berta cut Heather off before she completed her sentence. "Well, you thought wrong! Where is Romero?" Miss Berta announced distastefully.

Miss Berta looked outside the tall window and saw a small airplane land in downtown Thompson Square Park, three helicopters followed. New York security officers, NYPD blocked off the park in preparation for the landing of the designers. Miss Berta stomped around the office in her flats. "They're here! Heather, work on your poses, you look like you're laying eggs!" Miss Berta belted as Heather sighed deeply.

Heather Tilling's attire consisted of a long black dress with a mix of yellow and pink polka dots. The accents made the fall season designs a risk for *Eloquent Fashion Magazine*. The V-shaped neckline and ruffles complimented the dress in an unusual way. Nevertheless, the black-heeled boots she wore, with bright neon orange lipstick, was diversely strange.

"Turn your head sideways and turn your heels a little bit to the right," Romero said, as he directed the models.

Heather followed Romero's instructions. She made the photographs fierce and striking.

Miss Berta observed Heather with crossed arms. "Heather! Didn't I already tell you how terrible you look! What were you doing yesterday? Your dark circles are scaring Romero!" Miss Berta shrieked.

"No Madame Berta, she needed some eye makeup to cover the dark circles," replied Romero while Miss Berta stormed off angrily. "Anna! Get some eye makeup on Heather's owl eyes, please!" Anna came running with a clipboard in her arms and a small briefcase at her side. She opened the briefcase and pulled out a whole heap of makeup supplies. The large black makeup case had beige, green, and caramel brown eye makeup. Anna pulled out the blue eye makeup and began to apply to the models' eyelids.

Miss Berta paced the runway eight times, examining the entire platform until it met her ideal of perfection. Though there was room for complaint, she pointed to the side of the red carpet. "Anna! Get some diamond-looking stones on each side of the red carpet!" Miss Berta ordered rapidly. Anna patiently nodded her head and ran off. Five minutes later, she arrived with a tall, thin brown-haired man who carried a big case of extra materials: stones and brushes. The brunet man opened the case and placed the shiny, diamond-style stones on each side of the runway's carpet. This was very unusual for the "nature tones" Miss Berta had in mind for the photo shoot. The staff did as they were told without a word in response. Nevertheless, they did not understand why Miss Berta decided to make a drastic change so suddenly, while the fashion design representatives witnessed this change. Miss Berta decided that the nature tone theme she had previously decided on was boring and depressing.

Her readers would be in shock because of the big change. They expected Miss Berta to use nature tones during the fall season because she always did, but this time, she decided she would make a drastic change. Nature tones would be a thing of the past.

As the man completed the task of placing the shiny stones on the runway's carpet, the runway lit up vividly, adding excitement to the set. The key lights, the main source of lights for any live production, shone brightly.

The time for the commencement of the photo shoot drew near. Miss Berta gathered her team around her. "I'll be back with Pierre Monet and the other nine design representatives, who will be featured in the magazine this month, so please don't embarrass me, and don't embarrass yourselves." Miss Berta announced to her staff, as she walked away wearily.

Heather crossed her arms, as she watched Miss Berta walk toward the building's exit. She began to pout. "Remind me why we do this?" Heather broke out in tears, due to her irrational sentiment.

Romero put down his camera. "What on earth are you doing, Heather? You are ruining your makeup!" Romero broke out in anger, repulsed by Heather's lack of concern for the photo shoot. Anna approached Heather with a makeup kit in her arms. "Heather, pull yourself together! Our careers are on the line!" Anna snapped at her.

Heather took a deep breath. "I just need a minute."

"A minute!" Anna and Romero yelled back at her. "Miss Berta and the designers are coming any minute!" Heather looked at Anna and Romero, while the technical team, lighting crew, hair and makeup, DJ, and backstage crew watched Heather's breakdown. Her behavior worried each of them.

Romero clapped his hands together, in order to get everyone's attention. "What are you doing, people? Get back to work!" Romero said to the *Eloquent Fashion Magazine* staff. The staff returned to their workstations.

Heather sighed and prepared herself once again for the photo shoot. She wiped her tears, and straightened up her clothes and posture. Romero picked up his camera while Anna went behind the scenes, to assist the backstage models.

The backstage models were annoyed by Heather's demand for attention. "Who does she think she is?" A frizzy-haired model remarked to the composed model standing next to her.

Miss Berta came bursting through the door, followed by a strange man wearing a long dark suit coat. He held a briefcase in his right hand. Pierre Monet, a fifty-five-year-old frenchman was the representative from Chantel Fashion, sat down comfortably in one of the seats that had been set out for the audience. The seats were of black and brown leather material and were arranged in alphabetical order. This allowed for the formalities that everyone invited would have a seat of their own, to witness the fall season photo shoot for *Eloquent Fashion Magazine*. Gluten-free sodas, juices, sandwiches, caviar, and water were displayed on a lengthy brown table behind each seat. The waitresses and waiters were remotely slim in figure. Their bones were clearly visible under their skin. Each of them had their hair coiffed backward. Their uniform consisted of white shirts and black pants. Miss Berta realized, in order to promote her magazine, her staff had to promote a wild image for this particular shoot.

Eight representatives walked in with notepads and pens in their hands. Each of them took their seats in the audience. Monroe, a blonde forty-year-old woman with a short haircut representing Moi Fashion, appeared in a purplish-pink cashmere sweater. Her eyes were deep blue. "Hallo, I am here for the photo shoot," Monroe announced in a strong french accent. Miss Berta directed the woman to one of the vacant seats. Monroe sat down and began writing in her little black notepad. It took at least an hour for the seats to be filled. The lights dimmed and the runway lit up brightly with pastel, neon lights. The diamond stones on the red carpet reflected onto the ceiling, making it look like a rainbow from the Milky Way Galaxy. Heather and the other models practiced their poses. Romero prepared all three of his cameras.

Miss Berta stood before the crowd confidently. "I would like to welcome all of you to our September issue photo shoot. My goal is to promote the different vibes of our city. My inspiration for this event came from graffiti, the urban punk style. I have ventured throughout New York City to capture different shades of color that I witness on a daily basis. I have decided to change the designers this year. I have chosen clothing that will brighten the fall season. The designers I am looking for to feature in *Eloquent Fashion Magazine* will have a flair for graffiti and luminous pastels. My team and I have worked long hours, day and night, to bring you the best show possible.

We want you to enjoy the show. Be thrilled that we are featuring your clothing in our magazine. If you need anything, my assistants are standing on either side of the carpet. Just raise your hand, and they'll be happy to help you. *Bienvenue!* Enjoy!"

The audience applauded as Miss Berta walked off the set. "Donald, music!" She announced. Donald the DJ played the first record, while Heather, the first model, walked out onto the runway with a bounce in her step. She posed at the end of the runway, while Romero and the other photographers took photographs of her from every angle. Heather paced herself, trying to stay on beat as she walked down the runway. Her arms swung past her waist. The black dress she had on was pink, with orange polka dots. "She represents Moi clothing," Miss Berta announced. Heather ended her runway walk and went backstage as the music continued.

A slim girl followed Heather as she cat-walked down the runway. Her mini green and blue evening gown was bright. She wore yellow shoes and a neon yellow pastel scarf, with dots on it. She walked onto the runway with a small handbag in her hand. At that point, Miss Berta began to introduce each of the fashion lines by name. "Here we have Aurora Designs," Miss Berta announced while one of the models lingered on the runway.

The audience of representatives watched with distasteful expression the following model. Her accessories were poorly assembled. She wore polka dot stripes with ripped, colorful prints of neon blue, neon pink, and yellow. Graffiti was drizzled over her clothing. The crowd squinted. The bright colors on the clothes were blinding. The audience scowled and booed, as the remaining models walked backstage to change clothes. Romero and another photographer, Max Bren, suddenly appeared. Max was a slim young man who wore glasses. His hair was coiffed neatly. He was Romero's aide for the photography department at *Eloquent Fashion Magazine*. He followed all his instructions. He followed the last model; who was to be photographed, but couldn't help but notice how displeased the audience became. The neon lights, orchestrated by the lighting crew, blinded their eyes.

Jolene walked onto the runway; she looked about nineteen. Her face was thin and her cheekbones were visible. Her legs were as thin as toothpicks. She entered onto the runway wearing black, tight zebra-print fitted pants and diamond studded silver heels. She modeled the clothing as professionally as she could, but she realized her clothing was blinding from the headlights above her. "Here we have Chantel Designs," announced Miss Berta as the young girl strutted down the runway. Her face was painted in graffiti designs. Romero and the other photographers snapped their cameras like paparazzi following famous actors and actresses. There were ten models remaining; each wore clothing that was not color coordinated. Each ensemble was mixed and matched, following the urban style Miss Berta had in mind. The ensembles consisted of splattered paint on white clothing, mixed with splatters of red, white, and blue.

Miss Berta felt something wasn't going quite right. She continued to watch the show alongside the audience. All the models wore designers from Chantel to Aurora couture; handbags, hair accessories, and jewelry complemented the ensembles. Miss Berta relied on the avant-garde style from everyday people, people she saw on a daily basis. Street fashion was the common trend in her vision. The audience continued to scrunch their faces as the models walked off the runway. By the end of the show, the audience did not clap. The silence felt uncomfortable for everyone in the room.

Miss Berta came to the realization that the audience was displeased toward the end of the photo shoot. Her heart sank as she witnessed the silent room. The models portrayed a sick demeanor. They walked the runway with atrocious color combinations. Each model filled the entire room with what a distasteful aroma, because of the exaggerations of their clothing.

The photo shoot came to a conclusion, as Monroe, the representative for Moi Designs, stood up and announced her opinion in a strong-accent. "How could you consider choosing some of these models for the Moi line?"

Miss Berta hesitated at this question. "I felt Moi was all about seriousness and off-the-edge fashion."

Pierre interrupted and shook his head in disappointment. "Absolutely not. If you were doing your research about our company, you would know that we are all about poise, sophistication, and subtlety. I am sorry, but Chantal cannot accept to be featured in *Eloquent Fashion Magazine*. The model ensembles were mixed and matched with extreme, vibrant colors. The lighting in this room was blinding my eyes!" Pierre stormed off toward the exit while Miss Berta's jaw dropped. The other representatives watched the scene and began to slowly disperse toward the exit. Miss Berta's line of security,

Xenox, Lex, and Moe, restrained the crowd from causing uproar. The audience exited. Xenox approached Miss Berta. He had noticed her unease when Pierre Monet left the room. He instructed Lex to keep the audience under control. Lex relayed the instruction to Moe, through his headpiece.

Monroe continued to stand up. "Me too. I am sorry, but these models look like dogs when they are supposed to look like cats!" Monroe crossed her arms obliquely. "The entire show lacked color coordination. I could not stand the models, with graffiti painted on their faces!" She snapped, while she stood up before the remaining audience and explained that the models were not striking enough, which would give the clothing a bad reputation. Monroe stormed off, snatching her handbag and tailcoat. The remaining representatives threw out a slur of negative comments.

Monroe agreed with the representatives from the Chantel and Aurora. The other seven representatives had left the room, without a word of explanation. These three left were the only representatives who voiced their opinions, "I'm sorry." The remainder representatives from Moi, Chantal and Aurora grabbed their jackets and stormed off toward the exit, briefcases in their arms. Representative after representative diminished the large crowd, which flocked from the room. The photographers took pictures of the people leaving. As the crowd left, Miss Berta felt appalled. She did not expect this abrupt change for this photo shoot, to affect her entire fashion career. She did not have time to think of the consequences.

The room was trashed with food from the snack bar displayed on the floor. Romero was disappointed with the outcome of the show. He was exhausted; he and the entire staff alike did not believe what they had witnessed. It was the first time in history this happened to the magazine. Miss Berta's face had a heavy, saddened expression, as she was disgruntled because of the outcome. The employees from *Eloquent Fashion Magazine* voiced their opinions for the first time, describing each of their individual concerns. This shocked Miss Berta.

"An unsuccessful show," Romero contagiously announced.

"Perhaps I should have invested more time and energy," Miss Berta expressed as she looked upon the faces of her team. She especially looked toward Romero for emotional support. "What do you think happened

Romero?" She asked with anxiety. The question boggled her mind: What was she to do?

Romero, in his strong European accent, spoke calmly and collectively. "Excessively edgy, Madame Berta. You fell short this time. The graffiti concept was exaggerated. Not to mention the lighting; it blinded me as I was photographing the models.

"You can easily fix it; that is why I hired you," Miss Berta replied.

Romero continued, "The abrupt change from nature tone to graffiti was a big weight on all our shoulders. We all anticipated nature to be the theme, not graffiti. I remember you sending me that picture of that rose, which was painted in graffiti, but we always do nature in September. That threw the entire staff off the routine this month."

Miss Berta glared at Romero, who was exasperated at this point and out of breath. It was the first time he'd expressed his opinion to her without restraint. The remaining employees watched the dynamics of the power struggle begin to change as a result of the photo shoot. Miss Berta slowly expressed her rationale to her team. "Everyone, gather around. We have to start over, to win back their favor." The employees circled around Miss Berta, while silence swept across the room.

2

BAD PRESS

Bright colors and punk style was the future for *Eloquent Fashion Magazine*. It was the direction of Miss Berta's current fashion sense, for now and for the future. Flamboyant, ostentatious style was the remedy she had for the fashion industry. The street style she imposed was a form of decadence, revealed in the September issue of *Eloquent Fashion Magazine*, which circulated the streets of New York City. Young women and men gathered in flocks at corner stores, pharmacies, and small boutiques to collect the new issue. Street photographers documented the magazine's fan base. It consisted of college, high school, and middle school students, adult women, and some men, but very few. Usually, Miss Berta invited her fan base from outside of the *Eloquent Fashion Magazine* building into the lobby.

Gustave Vero, a well-known independent journalist and photographer, was Miss Berta's worst critic from the press. His background was in street journalism and photography. He took notes and photographed the screaming people, who represented the skateboarder, urban-punk style Miss Berta showcased in her magazine. Hiding behind a large oak tree, taking snapshots as the crowded scene of people flocked around like sheep for the launch of the magazine, Gustave looked mysteriously suspicious.

Miss Berta exited the brightly colored lit *Eloquent Fashion Magazine* building, as the crowd went wild with excitement. A young boy and girl approached Miss Berta, as she walked away from the building.

"Berta, we from Germany. We love you!" They yelled out in strong German accents. Holding hands, they pushed by the crowd, knocking other small groups of people over with their persistence. The young girl, who looked about eighteen years of age, stuck out a pen for Miss Berta to sign her magazine. Miss Berta took off her beige glove and took an ink fountain pen from her small pouch purse. She gently signed her signature in cursive on the August issue of the *Eloquent Fashion Magazine*, which was in the girl's hand. The words were written in black ink, which covered the legs of a model on the front cover of the magazine. The young girl repossessed her magazine. She waved at Miss Berta. As she began to walk away, she placed her dark sunglasses over her eyes, while waiting for her male counterpart to get his copy signed.

The next day, Miss Berta was on her way to work. Sixty-Eighth Street was busier and more chaotic than usual. As Miss Berta passed the newspaper stands, her eyes were filled with shock as she noticed the headlines.

BERTA LONDON'S MULTI-EMPIRE CRASHES!
Berta's Shocking Fashion Photo Shoot
Miss Berta's fashion shoot was repulsive, many of her critics proclaimed yesterday. Gustave Vero, her worst critic, believes she has defamed the fashion industry because of her punk, urban risk to be edgy. Gustave believes this to be the end of Ms. Berta's career in the fashion world, due to the fact that many of the top representatives walked away from investing in *Eloquent Fashion Magazine*.

An image of Miss Berta was included to the left of the article. She ducked into the *E.F.M* building just as she spotted another newspaper with a similar image on its front page. She decided to rush back on the street once more. Home was the only thought in her mind, as she walked past the hordes of photographers, including the repulsive Gustave Vero, who was taking snapshots. The press was ruthless; newspapers flooded the streets. All the newspaper and television stations covered the story of Miss Berta's photo shoot gone wrong.

The following morning, Miss Berta scolded her staff in the meeting she had organized. A strange man entered the conference room, where the meeting was being held. "What are you doing here?" Miss Berta asked, not knowing who this man was.

"I work for you," the strange man, in a top hat with long stringy hair hanging down to his shoulders, responded.

The *Eloquent Fashion Magazine* staff looked at him puzzled. They did not recognize him. Heather leaned forward toward Romero and whispered, "I don't recall him ever being employed here."

"Perhaps he's one of the new employees," Romero responded.

"Perhaps." Heather fell back in her seat, as did Romero. The strange man stood against the wall and listened intently, as Miss Berta proceeded with her discussion.

"What happened?" Miss Berta asked as she held up one of the newspapers, which was responsible for the libelous comments.

"Miss Berta, I think we went too far with the street edginess," replied Heather. Miss Berta was in disbelief at Heather's forward statement. Miss Berta opened the cover to her vanilla yogurt and began to eat it, ignoring Heather.

Meanwhile, Romero was flustered as Ms. Berta glared at him. "What do you think?" She asked.

"I concur," Romero announced. Miss Berta continued to look at Romero sternly. "Miss Berta, I never guide you wrong and you know that, but I must agree with Heather on this one."

"That's a first for you, Romero," announced Miss Berta. Romero, in anguish, immediately paused, then stood up abruptly. "I need a minute, I will be right back." Romero rushed out of the conference room, which had five large tables filled with staffers and people lining the walls. He rushed down the hallway, took the elevator to the ground floor, and hurried out the back door. He stood in a back alley, free of journalists and photographers. Romero paced outside the building, highly distressed. He took out a pack of cigarettes from his pocket, leaned against the wall, and lit his cigarette in an old-fashioned sort of way.

A few moments later, Heather pushed open the door. "Hey, Romero, Miss Berta would like to see you upstairs."

Romero took a deep breath. "I needed a minute."

"I know you do, we all do," Heather responded as she opened the door for Romero to enter the building.

Fifty staff members looked at them bewildered, when they entered the conference room. "Romero, where did you go?" Miss Berta asked, exasperated.

"I needed a minute," Romero responded.

"A minute! I am here trying to do damage control because of the bad press, and you are being nonchalant!" The entire staff watched the ongoing scene in silence. Miss Berta calmed her tone as Heather and Romero sat back in their seats. The entire staff listened intently as Miss Berta slammed the morning newspaper, with photos revealing the recent photo shoot from *Eloquent Fashion Magazine* on the table.

The magazine that lay on the table did not have its usual poise and decorum. The models posing on the front cover wore hats that covered their eyes. They had hands in their pockets and wore fiery punk red lipstick that was smudged around the mouth.

"Madame Berta." A slim man named Ricky raised his hand and spoke. "The entire show was a disaster." He could not help himself from expressing his opinion. He wanted to understand the cause of it.

"Ricky, you are here to do damage control. Make it all disappear." Miss Berta announced relentlessly. Ricky's eyes widened with shock at her request.

"I am working on it, but you must understand, the press is going berserk. They are not listening."

3

THE INCIDENT

Miss Berta was intent on delivering punishment. The young model Taureana had arrived at *Eloquent Fashion Magazine* on a one-year contract, a month prior to the disappointing photo shoot. She had a bubbly personality with good fashion sense. Her fashion sense was impeccably different. Her beauty was rumored to be like that of Cleopatra. Her open personality however, was unacceptable for the fashion industry. Her situation was ironic; she was let go because of being straightforward and honest with Miss Berta. Taureana carried herself in a stress-free manner. Miss Berta's hostility was unnerving for most of her staff. Taureana was called into Miss Berta's office that day for a review of her performance.

"Is modeling too much for you?" Miss Berta asked. Puzzled, Taureana was unsure of the question's purpose and meaning. "What's going on with you and the other models?" Miss Berta continued.

"I don't know what you are talking about," Taureana replied calmly.

"This is not about being gossipy, this is about your modeling photographs. They ruined the photo shoot," Miss Berta stated. Silence swept the room. Both Miss Berta and Taureana glared at each other, as they were the only ones in the room. Confused, Taureana did not know how to respond; she felt that she was open and followed the photographer's instructions, in regard to her model shots with her fellow models. Unaware that gossip circulated the building among Heather, Romero, and the other models, she figured what started out as friendly banter among the models had ended up as a highly dramatic situation. Romero, Heather, and the rest of the modeling staff were hostile. Gossip circulated about Taureana losing her spot on the runway.

Under Miss Berta's watchful eye, Romero was responsible for hiring and firing new models. In fear, Romero reported Taureana's model performances to Miss Berta. He discussed the conversations he had with Heather, Taureana, and the other staff members. Miss Berta was loud and obnoxious, because of the gossip that was circulating the building. This made it very difficult for her staff, especially difficult for Taureana.

Taureana greeted her fellow models regularly. Most of them were hostile in response, to avoid compromising their modeling careers. Miss Berta and the magazine were responsible for their careers. They could not be on her bad side. Romero and Miss Berta seldom replied to Taureana during her last days of work and when they did, it was a low-pitched, impersonal hello. Romero was in charge of *Eloquent Fashion Magazine*, once Miss Berta took off for vacations and holidays. The atmosphere in the office changed when she wasn't present. Romero created a peaceful environment. An environment the employees were comfortable with. They were able to relax, as well as gossip amongst themselves. Gossip propelled at extreme levels. It was encouraged by Miss Berta and Romero to gossip. They were curious about the personal lives of the models, as well as their opinionated ideas toward the industry.

This created a hostile work environment, and it was toxic. Inside the meeting rooms, conversations consisted solely of social media websites and the staff. Romero got personal with the models about their lives. This gave him the opportunity to be Miss Berta's favorite pet.

Taureana stood alone in the dressing room; she was under constant supervision by Romero and Miss Berta and the other models, who served as their spies. They reported on her daily activities at *Eloquent Fashion Magazine*. The other models used this to their advantage. Constantly fearful of being terminated from their contracts, this enabled the models to act despicable. The pressure was immensely intensified for Taureana, as she was in competition with the other models to keep her runway spot on the runway. Nevertheless, she was blamed for the failed photo shoot.

Her fellow models rolled their eyes at her as she passed by them, while saying hello. Confused of what was said in gossip, she felt she couldn't confide in anyone in the fashion world. She was called into Miss Berta's office, while Romero was present.

"Perhaps modeling isn't where you need to be," Romero said to Taureana, who was shocked. She placed her hands to her mouth and let out a deep breath to exhale her frustrations. "There's nothing I can do, the photo shoot went wrong, and the top industry officials are making complaints that their designer clothes were not represented adequately," Romero added.

"You can't expect me to be one hundred percent perfect. I know I haven't been the nicest, easiest person to work with because I am a perfectionist, but that shouldn't affect me as a model," Taureana replied.

"Well, it affected our business. We have no room for people who are not doing what they are told. Instead, you find you have the authority to gossip and give out orders, plus your modeling has been marginally mediocre and Miss Berta is not pleased with your overall performance," Romero replied as he thought to himself for a brief moment and then wrote the conversation they had on a blank white sheet of paper. "You have to sign this to end your contract," Romero said, while Miss Berta stood idle without issuing one word to Taureana. Taureana glanced at Miss Berta, who looked away with disregard. She was quiet the entire time.

"I'm not signing it!" It took Taureana a while, before she decided to sign her name on the dotted line. She was fed up with how the staff at *Eloquent Fashion Magazine* treated her. Their attitude toward her was once positive, but that was gone. She left the office after ending her fashion contract. Romero followed her outside Miss Berta's office downstairs and out of the building. Upon walking down the hall, he followed her downstairs, to exit the building. Taureana was infuriated at the sight of him. "I'll come with you to get the rest of your things." Romero said.

Taureana simply replied, "No, thank you! You let me go. I have nothing else to say." Taureana exited the building without looking back. The remaining staff witnessed the incident. They grew afraid of losing their careers. They did not want to stick around for the unexpected. They too, exited the building. Romero scolded them on their way out.

Two Weeks Later, Taureana Goes Back Home

The apartment, twenty blocks away from *Eloquent Fashion Magazine*'s head-quarters, was bare. It had nothing, except two suitcases on the floor. Taureana began to roam around the apartment for the last time. She had to make sure nothing was left behind. She was satisfied; everything was accounted for. She took her large-screen cell phone out of her pocket and began dialing. As she heard the phone ring twice, a warm voice answered.

"Hey darling, I'm glad to hear from you. You never call," the woman on the other line announced. Taureana restrained her tears.

"I'm coming home mother." She announced, as she hung up the telephone.

4

MISS BERTA'S HOUSE STAFF QUIT

That same day, Miss Berta arrived home to her luxurious mansion. The failed photo shoot was one of the worst days she witnessed. Meanwhile, her home staff: Chef Cephas and the two housekeepers, Alexis and Christine, were at the front door of her home. They had their bags packed. Cephas sat on his small suitcase of kitchen supplies. Christine stood there in a blue-and-white-striped dress. Alexis had his arms crossed, waiting.

Miss Berta approached them at the front door. She wore a burgundy dress with brown flats, which she wore with knee-high socks. Cephas immediately stood up. He had a nice new styled haircut, which was nicely shaped.

"Nice haircut," Miss Berta commended him.

"Thank you, madam. It isn't usual for you to give compliments." Cephas announced in his French accent.

"What is going on here?" Miss Berta asked hastily, as she put down her brown briefcase and crossed her arms. Christine and Alexis could not help themselves, as they both glared at each other with displeasure. Cephas took a deep breath as he took Miss Berta inside the house. Miss Berta continued to look at each of her staff with trepidation.

"We have not been paid Madame Berta," Cephas announced.

"Whatever are you talking about?" Miss Berta replied.

"Payments for our services have been delayed, Madame Berta, therefore we have no choice but to leave. We can no longer work for you."

Miss Berta was in deep shock at Cephas's bold statement. She was dismayed, as she saw Alexis and Christine nod in agreement.

"I cannot believe each of you have decided to end it this way," Miss Berta announced. Meanwhile, Christine approached Miss Berta to aid Cephas, who had run out of things to say.

"Miss Berta, we mean no disrespect, but we feel until you decide to compensate us for our days of employment, we cannot continue to work for you," Christine confided, as Alexis nodded his head in agreement.

"Not you too," Miss Berta exclaimed. Meanwhile, Christine and Alexis began to exit out the front in tears. They reflected on the number of years they had put into cleaning Miss Berta's home. They were going to miss their place of work. They were also going to miss working for Miss Berta. Altogether, each of them had worked for her for ten years.

Cephas was the last staff member to leave the home. He began to shed a tear. He no longer could restrain himself. He followed Alexis and Christine and did not say another word as he exited the front door. He got into the taxi with Alexis and Christine. The taxi drove off. Miss Berta watched all three of her former house staff leave her at her front door. It began to dawn on Miss Berta that her life would never be the same.

5

LIFE AFTER FASHION

The following day, Miss Berta entered her office, sat down, and noticed a pile of letters on her desk. Miss Berta read a letter from Monroe.

> *Dear Madam Berta,*
> *I apologize, but our company cannot continue to endorse Eloquent Fashion Magazine. Due to the September launch photo shoot, our company is displeased. We wish Eloquent Fashion Magazine the best of luck.*
> *Sincerely,*
> *Monroe Catalack*

Heather and the other *Eloquent Fashion Magazine* staff were outside of Miss Berta's office, waiting for her to speak at the staff meeting. They all pondered what to do.

Heather ripped off the expensive accessories that were displayed in her hair. She threw each of them on the ground in rage. "Good riddance!" She shouted while Miss Berta looked at her in disbelief.

"What on earth are you doing? You are the main cause for this. After all, it is your fault the magazine is sinking!"

Heather wiped off the vibrant makeup from her face. She continued to throw the accessories on the floor, while Romero held her back from her aggression. "You are the crudest, most ruthless and heartless person I have ever met! And you know what? I feel sorry for you. You have no family! I have ended up in the hospital countless times losing weight, because of you telling me I look like Hippo Heather! I am sick of your criticism. You are the worst boss, and I no longer work for you." Heather said, as she stormed off, while Romero chased after her, while she called over her shoulder, "You failed Berta. This is your magazine. The direction was yours. The models you chose are yours. The color combinations were all your doing."

Miss Berta watched attentively, while she overheard the conversation between Heather and Romero in the corridor. Heather belted out her feelings of frustration. "Just leave me alone Romero! I'm going home to my family. I have a three-year-old son," Heather announced as Romero released his grip from Heather's arm. The remaining staff looked at one another with amazement, gasping. This news threw them off the edge. It was unheard of for any model from *Eloquent Fashion Magazine* to have a child.

"I never knew she had a son," Miss Berta said to the remaining staff in disbelief.

Heather's temper boiled with anger. "It's her fault. This vision was hers! We did everything she instructed us to do for the magazine. She wouldn't accept our opinions."

Heather panted as she expressed her emotions. The team watched in amazement as Miss Berta stood motionless, with no emotion on her face. She turned to face her team, who were hanging in the balance, unsure of what to do. "I apologize for taking all of you away from your families. If you ever need a work-related recommendation, I hope I'll be in a position to help you in that regard. Good luck in your future endeavors, and I thank you." Miss Berta said.

After her bleak announcement, Miss Berta gave some thought to what Heather had said. The remaining staff feared their jobs were on the line. They looked distraught, while they nodded their heads to agree with Miss Berta.

The next day, Miss Berta went to visit Heather in Brooklyn. Brooklyn homes and apartments were built for humble, working class people. As Miss Berta approached the green doorstep, she knocked on Heather's wooden front door. Heather opened the door with her son, a round-faced, pink-cheeked boy named Taylor, whom she held in her arms. Taylor was in her arms. She was shocked to see Miss Berta at the door and gasped with disapproval.

"What are you doing here Berta?" Heather snapped. "I don't work for you anymore." She said, while Miss Berta tried to hand Heather a black portfolio. "What is this?" Heather asked.

"I wanted to have a word." Miss Berta responded.

Heather opened the door to let Miss Berta inside her home. She put Taylor in his wooden crib. "You have a beautiful boy." Miss Berta announced. Heather looked up at her in amazement. Silence swept the room, as they both looked at the little child in his comfortable crib. He smiled at them with his pink cheeks, as he played with his safari animals. "Thank you, he's all I have." Heather replied hastily.

"I apologize for my malicious treatment toward you. You must know that I had a business to run. In matters of business, nothing is ever personal. I've always admired how you were able to smile even after I would call you Hippo Heather. I wanted you to be miserable as I was. I guess I'm jealous of your happiness. I have lived selfishly, and I never realized you had a son. I never cared about what was going on in anyone else's life but my own. I apologize Heather. I made this for you and the other models. It's a portfolio with professional photographs of your modeling career from all the previous years you and the others, who worked for me." Miss Berta stood up, while Heather didn't say a word. Miss Berta picked up her belongings and left, as she walked down the front steps, she realized giving the portfolio was the nicest action she had ever done for anyone. She smiled to herself.

Months passed since Miss Berta decided to put *Eloquent Fashion Magazine* out of business. The magazine was loosing money rapidly. Due to her decision, Miss Berta was currently jobless. She applied for jobs at every fashion magazine throughout the city, and with the designers Moi, Chantel, and Aurora, she couldn't seem to land a job equal to that at *Eloquent Fashion Magazine*. Some days, she became more desperate than others. As the days drifted on, she applied for lower positions in the industry. In the meantime, Miss Berta's mansion was up for sale. She had buyers who were interested in the property. Her highest bidder was Ned Robinson, a man who worked on Wall Street. He was starting a family and needed the extra rooms. The contracts were signed and Ned Robinson was the new owner of Miss Berta's property. He was also the owner of her two bulldogs. Miss Berta sold her two dogs with the house. Her Separation from them was not easy, but she did it and had no choice but to move on. This new transition in her life could not accommodate her dogs.

Her new apartment rent was currently $1,900 a month, a big downgrade from her old mansion's mortgage payment. Miss Berta was in desperate need of the money. When she first moved in, she saw egg yolk stains on the windowsill. As she was cleaning them, the landlord walked in and introduced himself in his strong New York accent.

"Welcome to Liberty Towers." The landlord placed his right hand in front to shake Miss Berta's hand. Miss Berta stood, puzzled, and faced the man. "This is temporary for me." She said, while the landlord spoke up. "Glad to hear it. Your type are one of the worst I have encountered, "former rich' clients." His tone was hostile. Miss Berta did not respond. Instead, she paced back and forth, thinking about all the information that had been presented to her. The landlord became impatient. "Would you make up your mind, I haven't got all day!" He did not tolerate Miss Berta taking her time to make a decision. Miss Berta and the landlord finalized the official paperwork for her new home. They both signed the documentation.

Miss Berta sat in her new apartment sipping English Earl tea, while she read an article online from the *New York Times*. She scrolled to the job listings page in the classifieds section, where she stumbled on an advertisement for a nanny position. Her eyes were fixed on the $1,500-a-week headline.

Now, three weeks later, Miss Berta sipped her tea, as she continued to read the *New York Times* on the job listings, cultural and fashion side of the newspaper. The ad for the nanny vacancy was still visible on the online classified section of the newspaper. This made her believe that destiny spoke to her indirectly. The ad on the online newspaper was the push for her to act upon this drastic career change later in her life. She filled out her online application for Cedar College; a small college for aspiring teachers, located in a small, quiet town in upstate New York. Miss Berta received a full ride scholarship to attend Cedar College fulltime, due to her impeccable résumé. She commuted to the college from upstate New York. Due to the fact that she was not working a job at this time, she was depleting her savings to pay her rent. Her incentive was also to honor her late father, whose portrait hung on the wall above her office desk, where she had been reading. She reflected on the time her father supported her dream of teaching. The application, clearances, résumé and work experiences had been sent online through the college website.

Her first class at Cedar College started during the winter semester. Miss Berta wore her brown plaid outfit with beige shoes to her first class. She was the first one to take a seat. At 7:55 am, young people started flocking into the classroom for the 8:00 am morning class. At this point, Miss Berta felt out of place. She felt she did not belong. The student's ages ranged between eighteen and nineteen. The students began to snicker among themselves, because Miss Berta was the oldest in the class. They were clueless and had no interest in her as a person. Miss Berta could tell by the way they dressed themselves. They did not know who she was, and she found that a relief. She could not bear to be asked about *Eloquent Fashion Magazine*'s failure, nor questioned regarding where her life was headed.

The students stared at her curiously, but when the classroom door opened, they fell silent. A woman entered and Miss Berta recognized her instantly. It was Mrs. Whitmore, her previous nosey neighbor from the Upper East Side. She immediately dropped her briefcase. It took her a few moments to accept the fact that Miss Berta was seated in the third row in the classroom. Miss Berta maintained her composure and listened, as Mrs. Whitmore placed her briefcase on the teacher's desk and stood up.

"Hello class, welcome to Foundations of Teaching 100. My name is Mrs. Whitmore and this class is for those in the certificate program," she announced as she handed out the syllabus to the class, while she skipped over Miss Berta. Miss Berta remained silent and contemplated why she had not received a syllabus. Mrs. Whitmore passed around a sign-in sheet.

"Please do not forget the sign-in sheet." She announced, as the last student in the last row signed his name. He got up from his seat and put the paper on her desk. As she stood up and went through the entire syllabus, she allowed students to ask as many questions as they deemed fit. Miss Berta was silent through the entire process. The time began to approach nine o'clock and Mrs. Whitmore began to wrap things up.

"All right class, you may leave. We will continue next time." The students began to exit the classroom, to head to their next class. Meanwhile, Miss Berta stayed behind and approached Mrs. Whitmore's desk. She was in the process of putting her books in her briefcase.

"Yes, Miss Berta. What are you doing here?" Mrs. Whitmore proclaimed.

Miss Berta humbled herself. "I am in your class to get a teaching certificate."

"I know what happened concerning the downfall of the magazine, I know you sold your house and moved, but what I don't know is why you are in my class." Mrs. Whitmore said.

"I want to do something different, I made this promise to my late father as a child, that I would one day help children. My failure means destiny is speaking to me, that I should go in another direction. I need your help," Miss Berta confessed.

As the days passed, Mrs. Whitmore instructed her students on how to write formal papers and structure their paragraphs. Miss Berta had no problems with the theoretical classes. Nevertheless, she did become nervous, that the student teaching program would follow in a few months. Student teaching was part of the teaching certificate program she was pursuing, and a requirement for graduation. Mrs. Whitmore did give Miss Berta a hard way to go. She gave Miss Berta more homework than everyone else.

"You have three papers to write by the end of the week, eight pages each." Mrs. Whitmore announced before the students.

"That's not fair," Miss Berta replied. Mrs. Whitmore did want Miss Berta to succeed, so she challenged her and guided her along the way to fulfill the requirements to graduate.

Months and months passed and Miss Berta's student teaching date approached. She was required to serve as an aide for a public middle school. Her main duties as a student teacher were to assist the main teacher and put theory into practice. Miss Berta struggled with the students. They never listened to her instructions, nor did they respect her. The students continued to challenge her. Nevertheless, time went on, they grew to like Miss Berta, but still considered her a snobby lady.

Miss Berta completed her certificate program in June. All of her required coursework had been handed in right on schedule.

"Well, I knew you would have no trouble completing the program." Mrs. Whitmore said, as she handed her the certificate.

"Why did you make it challenging for me?" Miss Berta asked.

"I had to make things challenging for you, you are the oldest in the class. I just wanted to apologize to you. I am aware that I wasn't the easiest neighbor back then. It was out of line for me to spy on you. I also wanted to say, I'm sorry about *Eloquent Fashion Magazine.*" Mrs. Whitmore replied, as Miss Berta nodded her head in agreement. Miss Berta accepted her apology and gave her a hug. The small graduation ceremony drew to a close.

"I wish you the best, you have all the skills you need to succeed in the field of education." Mrs. Whitmore announced, as Miss Berta waved to her fellow students and teachers, who shared the classroom with her for the past six months.

Miss Berta finally transitioned into the nanny vacancy. Although she wasn't using her teaching credential, she wanted to take the initiative and try something new, working with children. Miss Berta was not very acquainted with children. She wasn't sure if she would like the job, but she wanted to try it. In her old neighborhood in Manhattan, there was nothing but rich, spoiled children who received everything they wanted, who acted like brats. Her thoughts toward them were negative.

It was Sunday night, Miss Berta slept on the idea of becoming a nanny. She tossed and turned, looking at the ceiling. She contemplated the idea. "Maybe it wouldn't be too bad," she whispered to herself. "After all, children are afraid of me." Miss Berta reached over the lamp seated on her side table and switched off the light switch.

Mr. and Mrs. Williamson were cosmopolitan people, thoroughly enjoying the city. They frequently attended social gatherings, constantly making appearances, especially at the Vixen Luxury Apartments in Manhattan, the most lavish hotel of all time. The night was young; the jazz instrumentalists played jazz music for the entire event. Mr. and Mrs. Williamson danced the night away in each other's arms. Most of the uptown community consisted of wealthy folks who had children left at home with their nannies.

Mr. Williamson pulled his wife closer. "Do you think the children are alright with the babysitter?"

Mrs. Williamson smiled. "There's nothing to worry about. We pay good money for their care."

Mr. Williamson simply noted, "It is unfortunate that we haven't found a caretaker who is willing to stay for a durable amount of time."

Mrs. Williamson put her arm around her husband's shoulders. "I guess you're right," Mr. Williamson agreed.

The following day, Miss Berta called Mr. Williamson on his cell phone, but there was no response. Ted Williamson was in the sales industry. He was a well-known businessman, accomplished in the state of New York. The landline phone rang and Mrs. Williamson answered. The voice on the other line spoke in a low, serene voice. "Hello my name is Berta London, and I am interested in the vacancy for the nanny caretaker position; the one that was posted in the newspaper." Miss Berta paused for a brief moment.

"Hello Berta, my name is Moira Williamson. My husband and I are looking for a nanny. I have three children who attend private school. My husband and I are in desperate need of your services." She replied.

Miss Berta listened attentively without interruption. "This is my first nanny job. I have never considered such a position."

Mrs. Williamson interrupted. "Why do you feel that you are the best candidate for this position?" She asked, as she took a deep breath. "My persistence," she replied briefly.

"I would like to set up an interview with you. Please come to the house tomorrow. The address is Eighth Avenue at Saint Marks Place, 10001" Mrs. Whitmore instructed. Miss Berta was excited to receive her first teacher opportunity, after completing her certification.

Miss Berta took a deep breath, to clear her throat. "All right Mrs. Williamson I shall see you tomorrow." She said, as she hung up the phone.

The following day was the interview; the sun was shining bright in the sky. Miss Berta left her home at 8:00 a.m. sharp for her 10:00 a.m. appointment with Mrs. Williamson. She arrived at the extravagant home and rang the doorbell. She heard screaming coming from the inside of the house. A butler wearing a name badge, WINSTON answered the door. At the entrance hall, a little boy ran past with streamers in his hand. Shocked at the boy's behavior, Miss Berta eyed him with disapproval.

"You may enter madam." The butler announced. Miss Berta entered the front room of the house. The floors were made of marble. The walls of the house were made of stone. The house was brightly lit. The beige curtains were thin as the wind blew them. Miss Berta observed the lobby. She noticed the rooms in the house were interconnected. She took a seat in the living room, while the butler instructed the little boy to settle down and control his composure in front of company. Winston was an elderly British man, who carried himself with poise and dignity. He was fairly short in height, with grayish-white hair. "Johnny! Come back here," he said. The butler turned to face Miss Berta and said, "Good morning madam, may I help you?" He said.

"Yes of course, is this the Williamson residence?" Miss Berta inquired, realizing she wasn't too far from her old neighborhood, during her fashion days. She recalled from her memory, Mrs. Whitmore mentioning the Williamson family, who were wild children, who lived a few blocks away. Meanwhile, Winston nodded his head and smiled.

"Indeed madam, indeed." Winston said, as he nodded his head.

"Well, I have an appointment with the parents." She replied.

Winston nodded in approval. "I shall get Mrs. Williamson for you," he announced. The rambunctious three-year-old, Johnny continued running around the living room. The butler finally caught up with him, holding him tightly so he wouldn't run. "Madam, would you wait a few moments, while I fetch Mrs. Williamson?"

"Not a problem," replied Miss Berta, while Winston exited the room.

Miss Berta sat down, waiting patiently. She daydreamed back in time to her high school days, and reminisced of an entire class laughing at her. A redheaded girl with short hair whispered to a group of four snobbish private school girls. "Her mother is ashamed of her. She would rather attend class than have to work with her mother, a fashion designer. Look at her hair, who wouldn't be ashamed?" The crowd of girls whispered amongst themselves. Overhearing the banter, a girl with unruly hair began to look down on her sketchpad. Professor Thornbush glanced at the drawing book, as the girl with disheveled hair drew miniature designs for clothes on her notebook. "I'm confiscating this." He said, as he rapidly picked up the book. "No wasting time in my classroom." He replied, while her book got taken away from her. The girl with unruly hair didn't say a word.

A woman with a short haircut, a gray long-sleeved dress with tape measure around the neck, knocked impatiently on the door of Mr. Thornbush's classroom. "I apologize for the disruption." The woman interrupted, as she looked at the girl with disheveled hair.

Miss Berta opened her eyes back to reality. A middle-aged woman, with a long braided plait entered the lobby to the Williamson home. She sat down comfortably on the large beige couch with her legs crossed.

"Welcome, I am Mrs. Williamson," she announced.

"Thank you." Miss Berta replied with patience.

"I would like you to tell me a bit about your background." Mrs. Williamson said with sincerity, while Miss Berta nodded her head.

"I have worked in fashion all my life and I have decided to make a career change." Miss Berta said, as she tried to hide her facial expression. Deep inside her feelings were hurt, she gave a sly smile to cover the pain.

"Well we will definitely need a nanny, who knows how to shop for stylish clothes for us." Mrs. Williamson replied with enthusiasm. This lifted Miss Berta's spirit. An idea sprung to her head immediately. If hired, she would introduce fashion to this high profile family. She was to be the nanny with the fashion sense. She smiled at Mrs. Williamson's enthusiasm.

"What else can you tell me about yourself?" Mrs. Williamson asked.

"I recently completed a certificate program in education." Miss Berta replied.

"Excellent. Why the change of careers?" Mrs. Williamson asked.

"It wasn't working out." Miss Berta replied modestly.

"Well, we need a nanny with your versatile talents. You would not be hired solely as the children's nanny. But, with your expertise in fashion, you would also be our family's personal shopper." Mrs. Williamson alerted.

Mrs. Williamson called out for her children to come downstairs and meet Miss Berta, their new nanny. Nick, a young boy of thirteen years of age, wore a t-shirt with turtle sneakers. He came down the stairs with a Turtle action figure in his hand. The turtle was a dark green color and dressed as a ninja. He looked at Miss Berta quizzically.

"Are you a Turtle fan?" he asked. Miss Berta didn't know how to respond to this question. She thought about it for a second. "No, I'm afraid not," she said.

Nick looked shocked; "I don't want you as my nanny! You don't like Turtles!" Nick belted. His mother interrupted him. "Nick, how many times have I told you not to judge someone, especially if they don't like Turtles?" His mother guided.

Mrs. Williamson apologized to Miss Berta and began to introduce her daughter; a sixteen-year-old high school teenage girl named Jessica, who was wearing sneakers. Her Eddie T-shirt was conspicuous. Eddie was an animated boy in a rock and roll band. It was a television series that many of the kids did not miss watching on television, and the brand was popular among teenagers.

Jessica's arms were crossed, and her bad attitude was clearly visible from across the room.

"Mom, I don't need another nanny! Look at what happened to the others! Can I go back upstairs, Eddie is on!" Jessica shrieked.

Miss Berta panicked. She put on the fakest smile possible as she greeted the children. Jessica rolled her eyes, while Mrs. Williamson announced each child's daily schedule.

"Johnny's three. He attends a private preschool and is one of the youngest and brightest children in his class. We are so proud of him. The only problem he has is that he gets hyper anytime he has candy. We give him candy to stop laughing at people for no reason. But then becomes a handful and throws loud temper tantrums, if he does not receive candy." Miss Berta nodded her head and scowled because Mrs. Williamson wasn't paying attention to her. She was calming little Johnny.

"Our little Nick is in the Scouts. He wants to learn how to make campfires like his peers, but we are proud of him nevertheless. We want him to be better than the other boys." Mrs. Williamson informed Miss Berta. Nick ignored his mother and continued to play with his turtle action figures. It was a method of escapism for him. He constantly felt neglected by his parents and other siblings. He read books or played outside in Central Park. Mrs. Williamson continued to share the family dynamic with Miss Berta.

The children detested the other nannies, who came before Miss Berta. She wasn't going to be any different. Midge Toma, a short woman, allowed the children freedom to pursue the activities of their choice. The day Johnny went missing was because she had to run to the cleaners for Mrs. Williamson.

Jessica went along; she had asked Jessica to watch Johnny at the playground, while she ran errands, but Jessica left Johnny unattended and Midge was cast away.

Rhoda Blitch, a past nanny for the Williamsons, was a woman in her forties who was caught at Casino Royal by Ted Williamson on the night she was supposed to be watching the children. She was also caught a few times stealing Ted Williamson's Frank Sinatra's, *The Golden Years* collection of music in their home.

The Williamsons were in dissension. They blamed each other for all of the nanny mishaps they had, which ended in disaster. The Williamsons desperately needed a nanny, one who loved children and had a background in education.

The children were detached emotionally from the nannies in the past, and wanted Miss Berta to quit as soon as possible. They disliked her, "stay away scowl," which she gave them on a constant basis.

"We have to get her like the others." Jessica whispered to Nick, infuriated that her mother had disrupted her show, which was on television.

"I can easily put a toad in her bed, while she's sleeping." Nick added.

"We can give little Johnny candy in the night, while she sleeps," Jessica replied enthusiastically. The children continued to listen silently as their mother asked questions and Miss Berta responded.

Because the children had a foul reputation around town, new employee prospects were not found. The nannies around town were unwilling to tackle the challenge. Mr. and Mrs. Williamson hadn't received much feedback from the advertisements they had placed in the newspaper for the nanny vacancy. Due to that effect, Miss Berta was fortunate to be hired as their new nanny-shopper.

"Are you going to ask me any more questions?" Miss Berta asked Mrs. Williamson as politely as she could. Mrs. Williamson turned to the children, who continued to stand quietly.

"Children, you may go back to your activities," Mrs. Williamson announced as the children scattered to their activities.

"No need, you seem like a sensible woman with an eye for fashion. You could easily pass for Miss Berta London, the fashion editor for the old *Eloquent Fashion Magazine*." Miss Berta looked at her in shock. "It isn't you,

you wouldn't be working for us if it was you." Mrs. Williamson giggled. Miss Berta gulped. Mrs. Williamson eyed Miss Berta from head to toe.

"It is you, I know it. I could never forget a face, and your name surely gives it away." Mrs. Williamson was beyond excited.

"Yes, it is. Fashion is no longer part of my life," Miss Berta replied, as she took out her certification in education. Mrs. Williamson glanced at it briefly.

"Well, welcome to the family," Mrs. Williamson announced gregariously.

Miss Berta quickly interrupted, "I accept the position under the condition that you do not reveal my identity to your friends or associates."

Mrs. Williamson nodded her head. "You have my word."

The following day, Miss Berta was hired. Jessica got into trouble for not wearing her school uniform. She wore graffiti cartoon–styled Eddie clothing instead. She was called into the principal's office. Principal Hunt threatened to call her parents, but Jessica insisted he call Miss Berta instead. Jessica attended the prestige Glendale High School, a Catholic high school. Principal Hunt was a chubby man with a grayish-black beard. He wore a red faded tie. The students always took advantage of his kindness. A few hours before class, one of the students snuck into his office, stole his lunch, and ate it. The principal was never able to get to the bottom of who the culprit was.

Miss Berta agreed to come in and speak to Principal Hunt, after she had received the message concerning Jessica. She got dressed in her business attire and was at Glendale High at her earliest convenience. She knocked on the administrator's office, as a lady in a polka-dot dress, with a brown jacket answered the door. The lady looked at her watch. "You are right on time Miss Berta. Principal Hunt is ready for you." She replied.

Miss Berta knocked on the door. A man in a brown suit answered. "Come in." He replied. Miss Berta entered his office. "Do sit down." He instructed, while Miss Berta sat down in one of the vacant chairs. "Greetings, Miss London. I have no choice but to suspend Jessica for missing classes, and not wearing her uniform." Principal Hunt announced.

Miss Berta took a deep breath. "Well, is there anything she can do, to get out of the suspension?" Miss Berta asked. Meanwhile, Jessica appeared in Principal Hunt's office.

"Right on time. Have a seat, young lady." He announced. Jessica's hair was disheveled. She placed her backpack on the ground next to the seat, where Miss Berta was seated.

"I know Principal Hunt. I was not wearing the uniform, and missed a few classes, but can't it slide?" Jessica insisted, as she was hastened to leave the office. Principal Hunt grew annoyed at her behavior. "Please, sit down!"He said firmly, while Jessica remained seated and listened patiently.

"What is causing you to miss your classes?" Principal Hunt inquired. Jessica looked up at Miss Berta.

"My band. I care about the music," Jessica responded sincerely.

"What about our uniform policy?" Principal Hunt inquired.

"Like I said, I am in a band and a few of our concerts are during the weekdays." Jessica replied politely.

"Well, if this continues, young lady, I will have no choice but to suspend you." Principal Hunt held a serious demeanor and Miss Berta and Jessica knew he would do it.

"It won't happen again." Miss Berta admitted, while Jessica grew annoyed. Principal Hunt smiled at Miss Berta's response.

"Well, nothing to worry about, since this will not happen again, and no missed classes. The school uniform is expected to be worn all the time on school property. You are also expected to bring up your grades. You are currently below average," Principal Hunt continued.

"She will bring up her grades." Miss Berta announced, as they both got out of their seats and exited Principal Hunt's office door.

"I am not dropping out of my band." Jessica initiated the conversation as they made their way home.

"What do I tell your parents? You will not drop out of the band, but you will limit your time playing to the weekends." Miss Berta insisted, while Jessica got into the Williamsons' white car, the one Miss Berta had driven to pick her up.

"Fine, I'll limit my time for the weekends, but you can't tell my parents," Jessica proposed. Miss Berta agreed to keep the close call suspension under wraps. She was sworn to secrecy.

As the lights went out in the Williamson home, Jessica checked her clock. It was midnight, when she slipped out of bed, already dressed in a white t-shirt and torn jeans. She grabbed her guitar, backpack and headed downstairs as quietly as possible. She accidentally dropped her guitar, which made a loud thud on the floor. Jessica picked up her guitar and tiptoed down the hallway. She entered the kitchen and spotted Nick with two of his friends. They were having chocolate chip cookies and glasses of milk in the pitch-dark. Shocked, Jessica dropped her bags.

"What are you creeps doing up so late eating cookies in the dark?" Jessica demanded, annoyed to see her brother crossing his arms.

"We should be asking you the same question," Nick contested.

"Go back to bed, Nick, and that includes the rest of you," Jessica muttered.

"You go back to bed, or I'm going to tell Mommy and Daddy. But this is your lucky night. Take us with you, and we'll keep quiet." Nick proposed, as his two friends chuckled. Time was running out, and Jessica had no other alternative but to consider Nick's absurd proposal.

"Fine." Jessica announced, annoyed at the fact that children who were thirteen duped her.

"Fabulous. Give us five minutes to assemble our things. Tommy, Earl, and I have to grab our bags." Nick confessed.

"No Nick. I don't have time for the delay. School is tomorrow and I don't want to be late for my rehearsal." Jessica growled.

"Perhaps Mommy and Daddy would like to show up to this rehearsal." Nick continued to blackmail Jessica.

"Fine, you little newt, but if you're not back in five minutes, I'm leaving without you." Jessica responded.

"Yeah...right. Come on. Tommy and Earl. Let's get our things."

Nick instructed his friends. Nick, Tommy, and Earl rushed upstairs.

"Sh...you creeps. You're going to wake everyone up." Jessica whispered. She sat down on one of the wooden stools in the kitchen, waiting for the boys. They finally reappeared, each of them dressed in his Boy Scout uniform.

"Let's go." Jessica whispered. They were heading out the front door when Little Johnny ran toward them, dressed and a backpack on his back. As Jessica was closing the door, Little Johnny interrupted her.

"I want to come, too." Little Johnny announced.

"Johnny, I told you, you can't come." Nick announced. Jessica did not say another word. She picked up Little Johnny and all of them exited the front door. Jessica opened the door to a minivan, which had been waiting for them. Nick and his two friends entered first, followed by Little Johnny. Jessica was the last to enter.

"Put on your seatbelts," Jessica ordered. The boys followed her instructions as Andre and Zyrock pulled out of the driveway.

"What are you doing? This is not *The Brady Bunch*," Andre belted at Jessica.

"Look, as I was sneaking out of the house, they followed me and threatened to tell my parents, if I did not bring them along," Jessica replied.

"Fine, Jessica, but it is your responsibility to keep them quiet." Zyrock replied.

Jessica was a talented guitarist. She loved her instrument; it was the only way she could express the bottled-up anger she had for her parents. Passionate about Elvis Presley and the Beatles, who were her influencers to sing. Her bedroom had posters of all the bestselling rock artists. She felt the band was her family. At home, she felt alone most days, never able to approach her parents with her problems. She played with her band, Knox, until 2:30 a.m. every night and then went to school the next day. Jessica had gotten her own apartment with the band in secret. Her parents were ignorant of this. She shared the place with the band members. They were eighteen years old and were able to get the apartment lease. Each band member had his own bedroom for comfort. Most of them got the rent money from their large allowance, which came from their parents.

Jessica took her two brothers and Nick and Johnny to the two upstairs bedrooms. They groaned with disappointment.

"Can't we watch you play, Jess? Please," Nick added.

Jessica looked at their hopeful faces and agreed. "Fine, but only for five minutes." They followed Jessica downstairs. The music equipment was hooked. Zyrock and Andre were rehearsing their voices, while they practiced their instruments. Jessica stood up and began to sing aloud, "You like me or you don't." The music instruments were pounding with rhythm along with Jessica's voice. Nick and Johnny began to touch the instruments.

"It's time for bed," Jessica interrupted an hour later, and escorted all of the boys upstairs.

"This is where all of you will be sleeping; we have two rooms with two bunk beds. Go to sleep and keep quiet. Nick, watch Johnny. Don't tell Mommy and Daddy." Jessica told to her brothers.

"What about Miss Berta?" Nick inquired.

"You definitely can't tell her."

"It's really awesome that you have a band." Nick said. Jessica smiled. It was the first time Nick had something nice to say.

"All right. Well, we are going to be practicing, so you might want to close the door." Jessica said to Nick. Nick nodded his head in agreement. Each of the children jumped into their bunk bed.

"Good night Johnny." Nick said to his brother.

"Good night, Nick, Tommy, and Earl." Jessica said.

Jessica went downstairs to find Andre and Zyrock, who were tuning their instruments.

"I guess we'll be practicing all night, thanks to Jessica." Andre grumbled.

"Look, Nick was up when I tried to leave, and of course he had his two best friends with him. Johnny followed." Jessica explained to her band members.

"Whatever; one, two, three, hit it." Zyrock announced as each of them grabbed their instrumentals, while Zyrock began playing the drums loudly. Andre was on bass guitar, playing softly, so he wouldn't wake the boys.

Miss Berta was at the Williamson home, a nervous wreck, pondering the children's whereabouts. Mr. and Mrs. Williamson were gallivanting at a neighborhood party, when the children went missing. It was her duty to keep them safe until their parents arrived. She called the police department. It was past midnight and the neighbor's houses were silent and dark. A police officer wearing a blue uniform was talking on his speaker system, while he took out his notepad and faced Miss Berta.

"Where did you last see the children?" The officer asked.

"There were in their rooms fast asleep." Miss Berta responded.

"Well, if they show up, give us a call. We will send out a search party." The officer replied and left. It was two o'clock in the morning. Mr. and Mrs. Williamson arrived home. Mr. Williamson was displeased to find his children not in their beds. Mrs. Williamson; did notice the new clothes in their closet space; and rummaged through Jessica, Nick, and Johnny's new wardrobe and smiled. She glanced over to their beds and noticed her children were not in them. She descended into the living room, to find her husband and Miss Berta already downstairs.

"Where did she go at this hour? It is your duty to know," Mrs. Williamson added, exasperated to find her children out of bed, while Mr. Williamson continued to glance at his newspaper, placed on the couch. This was his way of handling the situation.

Miss Berta stood in front of Mrs. Williamson. "I called the police, they sent out a search party." Miss Berta explained.

"Look, I appreciate you styling the children in fashionable attire. You are really good, I admit. You are the first nanny I have had to make a contribution to the family in that regard, but where are my children?" Mrs. Williamson belted. Miss Berta was overwhelmed. She did not know what to do. It was the middle of the night. Nick, Tommy, Earl, and Little Johnny grabbed their bags and jumped into the minivan, which Zyrock drove. As he pulled up the Williamson driveway, Nick, Jessica, and Little Johnny got out of the van. Jessica turned to Zyrock.

"Please drop off Tommy and Earl home." Jessica requested. Zyrock and Andre shook their head in agreement. They drove off. Nick, Johnny, and Jessica approached the front door to their home and entered, as quietly as possible.

Miss Berta sat in the kitchen as each of the children entered. "Hello Jessica. I am appalled at your conduct, and to add insult to misery, you have the audacity to involve your brothers in your nonsense." Miss Berta crossed her arms in disappointment. "Nick, take your brother upstairs."

Meanwhile, Jessica put her bags on the floor. She sat down on one of the stools next to the table.

"Now, your parents are still asleep, so they don't know about this,"
Miss Berta announced.

"What are you going to do?" Jessica asked.

"That depends on you, Jessica," Miss Berta replied.

"What is that supposed to mean?" Jessica inquired obnoxiously.

"This can't happen again."

"Or else?"

"What you did is very serious," Miss Berta replied.

"They wanted to come and I tried to stop them. Look, music is my destiny. I had to practice with the band for our upcoming performance." Jessica told her.

"Again, this cannot happen again. At least leave your brothers out of it." Miss Berta said.

"Does this mean that you're not going to report me to my parents?" Jessica asked.

"It means that I will help you adjust your schedule, so you don't attempt to do this again."

"You have my word." Jessica replied.

"Good. Now, get upstairs before I change my mind." Miss Berta reprimanded her.

Mrs. Williamson was in bed by the time the children had arrived home, but Mr. Williamson was still awake, with one eye open waiting for them. He heard the children head upstairs, while Miss Berta scolded them.

"Where are the other boys?" Miss Berta reprimanded Jessica.

Yawning, Jessica admitted. "Zyrock and Andre dropped them home."

"Good, all of you to bed now!" Miss Berta announced, infuriated, as they each went into their bedrooms. As the children entered their rooms, they noticed their closets had been altered. Jessica entered her room first. Her closet was open, revealing bright pastel shirts and pants. There was a note on the side of the closet, which read: "Don't mention it. You have to look the part, if you're going to be a rock-and-roll singer," signed, "Miss Berta." Jessica smiled. She appreciated this small token of support from Miss Berta. Johnny and Nick were amazed at their new clothing styles. Their clothes consisted of brown, white, and beige polo shirts with striped yellow, blue and green pants. Nick's clothing had him in awe; turtle action figures had been sewed onto each of his polo shirts. Miss Berta left a note, which read: "Have fun." The note was left on their closet door. Nick and Johnny smiled at the note and went straight to their beds and feel asleep immediately. Mr. Williamson heard Miss Berta descend from the staircase into the living room.

"Are the kids safe in bed? I came downstairs to wait for them." Mr. Williamson interrupted, yawning, as he glanced up from his newspaper. Miss Berta was shocked to find Mr. Williamson in the living room.

"Yes, they are." Miss Berta admitted.

"This doesn't happen again. It does, and you are out of a job."

Mr. Williamson announced sternly. Miss Berta nodded her head in agreement. Mr. Williamson got up from his seat and headed upstairs. Meanwhile, Miss Berta called the police department using the landline phone that was in the living room. The line rang and a deep voice picked up the line.

"New York Police Department. How may I help you?"

"I am calling from the Williamson household. My name is Miss Berta London and I reported five missing children earlier, they have all been accounted for. They are all safely home." Miss Berta said.

"Thank you." The voice on the other line answered.

Saturday afternoon, Miss Berta allowed Jessica and her band members to gather for practice at the garage of the house, where she could keep an eye on them.

Zyrock, Andre, and Jessica had known one another since ninth grade. They were seniors in high school, with big, deranged, egotistical personalities. Jessica was in the ninth grade when she sang for the talent show at school. It was one of her first performances. Zyrock and Andre were in the band, but they needed a singer for the group. Reluctant to have a girl in the band, they weighed the pros and cons. Jessica was fairly pretty. She would be beneficial to getting recognition for the band's music. She was outgoing, bold, and daring. The band appreciated her wild onstage personality. They needed these characteristics to complete the band. Jessica, Zyrock, and Andre set up the equipment, when a young man of twenty walked towards them. Jessica was shocked that this tall man was built like a football player, approached her at her home garage. "What are you doing here?" Jessica asked.

"I'm a business major in college," replied the young man.

"Interesting, I've actually seen you a few times at our concerts," Jessica said.

"Zyrock told me you would be here?" The boy admitted. Zyrock smiled.

"I know I should not have come, but he kept harassing me." Zyrock confessed to Jessica, while Andre was tuning his guitar.

"Technically, I have two abodes." Jessica said laughingly, looking up at him, bewildered.

"Why are you here? Aren't I a little too young for you?" Jessica asked.

Meanwhile, Miss Berta entered the room, suspicious of the new college student.

"What is going on here?" Miss Berta demanded. Jessica began to blush out of embarrassment.

"Well, I just wanted to come by and tell you that I like your voice a lot." The boy admitted.

Miss Berta interrupted the conversation, "I have to ask you to leave, young man," she insisted. The boy dismissed himself and left. Meanwhile, Zyrock and Andre were frustrated that their practice time was getting cut short.

"Jessica, are we practicing tonight or what?" Andre intervened.

"Let's rock, guys!" Jessica stood and ignored Miss Berta. Zyrock discussed their practice sessions. "Five hour practices daily should do the trick." He proclaimed.

"What about school?" Andre asked.

"Dude, our plan was to take music seriously and leave school." Zyrock explained sternly. Miss Berta stood to watch them.

"Absolutely not, Jessica! You are going to have to cut some hours to do your homework." She belted. Meanwhile, Johnny and Nick followed Miss Berta outside to the garage. "Miss Berta, are we having a party?" Nick proclaimed, tugging at Miss Berta's arm, while holding Johnny's hand.

"Absolutely, not. Why?" She belted.

"Look, Ber, look." Johnny instructed. Miss Berta turned to find a group of teenagers standing at the tip of the garage, in front of the house. The group of young teens began to increase in number. Miss Berta began to hold onto Johnny's hand. Nick crossed his arms anticipating Miss Berta's actions, who, was in the process of instructing the crowd to leave. But she couldn't help but glare at Jessica and the band; who were in a sad disposition. Jessica's face made Miss Berta reflect on her own youth, and her fashion days. She felt sorry for Jessica, she knew what it was like to have a passion and have parents never around to support it. She simply stood before the crowd, and fell silent and smiled. Zyrock, Andre, and Jessica were ready to practice before the crowd.

As night approached, Zyrock played the drums. Andre played the bass guitar. "One, two, three let's go, Jessica!" Zyrock indicated.

Jessica swooned her head to the rhythm, she moved from side to side, as Andre strummed to an eclectic beat, and Zyrock slammed on the drums. Jessica began singing: "Escape I will one day, beyond my fear, beyond my tears. Escape is my destiny; escape is my future. Let me escape from this wilderness."

Tears streamed down her face. The crowd of people clapped their hands together. The young man who had earlier come to talk to Jessica reappeared by the garage, impressed with Jessica's beautiful, harmonious voice. The crowd now consisted of about twenty-five people, who were wild with excitement. Watching her intently, the young man, Randy, began to smile. Randy stayed for the entire practice jam session and was in hiding, to stay and watch her play. Jessica smiled at him and waved, just realizing that he had been there the whole time. As the practice session came to an end, she slowly put down the microphone on the nearest table and approached Randy. The crowd of people began to disperse, as it was getting later and later, the bands were at the end of their practice session.

"Still here." Randy smiled at Jessica while he crossed his arms. "Well, I'm impressed, Miss Jessica. You can carry a tune, very impressive."

"Thank you, I appreciate that you enjoyed the show." Jessica turned to face the other band members. They laughed at the entire situation. "Are we staying here tonight?" Jessica asked, while Andre giggled then began to yawn, as he lowered his bass guitar to the floor anxiously. "I think you better stay home, Jessica, your grades are floundering compared to ours. We'll stay back at the apartment." Andre stated.

"I don't think getting D's in class reveals that you both are going to attend the Ivy Leagues or even get into a college."

"At least we're passing," Andre retorted.

"True," Jessica replied.

Andre and Zyrock laughed boisterously. They continued to mock Jessica. Jessica packed up one of her backpacks. Kneeling on the floor, annoyed at

Zyrock and Andre, while they were discussing their plans post high school. Jessica felt like an outsider. As she finished packing her microphone equipment into her backpack, Randy approached her, leaving Zyrock and Andre to their theatrics.

"I would like to see you again, if that is possible?"

Jessica, pleased at the proposal, began to smile. She hadn't participated in the dating scene during her entire high school life. There were guys she liked, but she never took the initiative to let it be known that she was interested. "Sure, we can hang out together as friends," Jessica replied.

"Is it too forward to let you know, that perhaps I would like to be more than friends?" Randy inquired as Jessica giggled to herself. She looked intently at Randy's earnest face. "I'm serious," said Randy. Meanwhile, Miss Berta was in the process of telling the teens to go home.

"It's all over! Go home, all of you! I will not say it again!" Miss Berta instructed the crowd. A mysterious boy at the edge of the group did not budge, however, Miss Berta approached him.

"You need to go home, kid." Miss Berta declared.

"My name is not 'kid.' It's AJ, and I don't have a home to go to." The boy admitted with sadness. Miss Berta's heart went out to the boy. She became curious and began to question the young teenager.

"Is this your first time, coming to Jessica's show?" Miss Berta inquired. The boy shook his head. "Not at all. I always show up and hear them play."

"Why do you come? Do you go to the same school as Jessica, Zyrock, and Andre?" Miss Berta asked.

"No, I live on the other side of town, where it's not as nice, but I saw a flyer for this band and I have been following them ever since." He confessed.

From the corner of her eye, Jessica saw the mysterious boy and waved. The boy waved back. It was rumored that the boy lived with his mother and a mean stepdad, but that was all the information they knew. The boy quickly faced Miss Berta and said, "Goodbye, miss," and walked into the darkness of the night. Jessica continued to talk to Randy. Zyrock and Andre picked up their equipment and left. Leanne was a short girl with a loud personality. She was also Jessica's best friend. Flyod, who was best friends with Zyrock and Andre.

Randy stayed behind to finish his conversation with Jessica.

"I do not participate in the dating scene." Jessica told Randy.

Randy was not going to accept no for an answer. He kept up with his persistence. Leanne dated Flyod while Jessica's secret relationship with Randy never started. Leanne was dropped off at her home. She kissed Flyod on the cheek in front of Zyrock and Andre and waved good-bye, as they drove away. Meanwhile, on the same night of the show, Leanne's cell phone began to buzz.

"It's over between Randy and I. I'm sorry." Jessica texted Leanne on her cell phone, feeling quite relieved she had done so.

"Look, we should double date, Flyod, me, you and Randy. Give Randy a chance. Your nanny was there. I felt awkward for you." Leanne text back.

It was ten o'clock in the morning. Jessica approached Miss Berta in the kitchen, as she was placing carrots, cheese, and cucumbers in the blender, while Johnny was seated on the floor next to her.

"What are you doing?" Jessica asked.

Miss Berta continued to chop the vegetables on the counter. "I'm making snacks for your baby brother."

"Do you think this will help his erratic behavior?" Jessica anticipated.

"It will have to." Miss Berta replied, completely focused on placing the vegetables in the blender.

"He's going to repudiate those kinds of snacks." Jessica confessed. Miss Berta refrained from chopping the vegetables and faced Jessica.

"Someone's been doing homework. That's the first time I've heard you use proper diction. I'm proud of you." Miss Berta proclaimed, while Jessica smiled.

"Great, but I need a favor," Jessica insisted.

"Well, you've been doing your homework, so I will grant the favor. What is it?" Miss Berta replied. "Oh, before I forget, who is that mysterious boy that was standing idle during your garage jam session a few days ago? He told me his name's A.J. Do you know him? I did see you wave at him, and he waved back at you."

"He's been coming to my shows for as long as I could remember, but I've never met him." Jessica responded.

"Rumor has it that he doesn't live anywhere close to this neighborhood. To be honest, I don't know that much about him," Jessica confessed.

"He said he didn't have a family to go home to." Miss Berta replied with sadness. "Anyway, what can I help you with?" Miss Berta questioned, switching the subject.

"I need you to take me shopping for my date tonight." Jessica excitedly admitted.

"A date with whom?" Miss Berta asked.

"Randy," Jessica admitted.

"Fine, but only because you've been dedicating time to your studies." Miss Berta agreed, while Jessica jumped to give her a hug.

"Thank you so much." Jessica responded humbly.

"We'll have to take your brothers." Miss Berta confessed

"Okay," Jessica agreed.

As midday approached, Jessica and Miss Berta were shopping in a small boutique called Classe. It was quite expensive. Miss Berta ignored the price tags and simply picked up several different ensembles. Meanwhile, Nick and Johnny were playing hide-and-seek in the clothing racks. Jessica was in the changing rooms, trying on subdued dresses, which were in navy blue and beige, with floral lace designs. Miss Berta was still picking out clothes for Jessica to try, when the sales representative approached her.

"Miss, I'm sorry to bother you, but you look like that fashion editor from *Eloquent Fashion Magazine.*"

"You have me mistaken sir." Miss Berta reassured him. Jessica appeared, holding the navy-blue dress and the beige floral dress.

"I love these two, but I cannot decide which one," Jessica admitted.

"The blue dress with the floral designs is yours. It brings out your eyes." Miss Berta blurted out.

"I agree," the salesman said, and Miss Berta tried to hurry him along.

"We'll pay for the navy-blue dress. Kids, wait here till I get back." Miss Berta instructed, and she followed the salesman to the cash register.

"That will be eight hundred dollars." He proclaimed. Miss Berta gave him her credit card. He began to read the name on it aloud. "It is you! It is!" He belted aloud.

"Ring me up now!" Miss Berta replied, infuriated. Taken aback, the salesman did as he was told and fell silent. He rang Miss Berta up, giving her back her credit card, and placed the dress in a shopping bag. Miss Berta quickly snatched the bag from him and returned to the children's side.

"Time to get home." Miss Berta announced, and they left the boutique.

It was seven o'clock in the evening and Johnny and Nick were in their rooms playing, while Miss Berta was putting the finishing touches on Jessica's hair. Jessica was already dressed in a floral mini-dress. As Miss Berta turned off the curling iron and completed Jessica's hair, she began to apply red lipstick on Jessica's lips.

"Smudge," Miss Berta replied. Jessica did as she was told and Miss Berta took out an eye shadow palette, and applied simple strokes to the top of Jessica's eyelids. The doorbell rang.

"You're done." Miss Berta confessed Jessica stood up, picked up her mini black shoulder purse. "How am I supposed to pay you back for the dress. I hope you didn't use your entire salary" Jessica confessed.

"I have some savings." Miss Berta smiled. "You best get going."

Funksway Italian was the name of the restaurant. It was considered a hot spot for well-to-do teenagers and those in their early twenties. The restaurant was lit with dim lighting and the guests were well dressed, seated at intimate tables. Jessica, Randy, Leanne, and Flyod were seated in a private suite with private service. Leanne was holding hands with Flyod, while scooping the last piece of food onto Flyod's plate. They both giggled. The waiter approached with separate checks for each couple. Leanne completed her fancy herbed pasta, while Flyod had already eaten the food that was on his plate. He took out his credit card, while the waiter walked away with it.

"Are you old enough to have a credit card?" Leanne asked him.

"Yep, there's credit cards for teens, didn't you know?" Flyod replied.

"I did not know that." Leanne admitted.

"Well, technically, you have to be part of your parents credit card account," Jessica said. "No wonder I don't have one. My parents will never put me on their credit card plan."

Leanne confessed.

Randy could not pay for both his and Jessica's meal. Though Funksway was affordable for people of an elite caliber, his parents were not in the same financial bracket as the rest of the group. The waiter approached them and handed Randy back his credit card, "Sir, your credit card was declined."

Leanne gave Randy an exasperated look. She was disgusted. Jessica was empathetic toward Randy.

"I'll pay for you." Leanne said aloud, so everyone at the table could hear. Randy felt embarrassed.

"I have enough money to do it, Leanne," Jessica said, and took out her card and handed it to the waiter.

Randy and Jessica sat and watched Leanne and Flyod flirt with each other. The waiter returned with Jessica's card.

"Thank you all for dining with us," the waiter declared. They each got up to leave.

In the large parking lot, Jessica sat in the backseat of a bronze Lexus with Randy, as the cool breeze blew in the window. Leanne entertained her date with bad jokes. Randy moved close to Jessica and placed his arm around her. Jessica giggled, as did Randy. Flyod started the car.

"All right, I'll drop the girls off first," he proclaimed.

"Agreed," Randy said as they headed out.

6

THE WILLIAMSON CHILDREN'S UPDATED REPORT

Mr. and Mrs. Williamson received their children's report cards. They grew concerned with Jessica's grades, which indicated that she failed most of her classes.

JESSICA WILLIAMSON
GRADE REPORT:

ENGLISH ADVANCED	A
ALGEBRA II	F
CHEMISTRY	F
PHYSICS	F
VOICE ADVANCED	A
P.E.	F

Mr. and Mrs. Williamson had no idea what was going on in Jessica's life. Both parents were too preoccupied with their everyday affairs, as they attended business parties most nights. Jessica felt ostracized by her parents.

One evening, Miss Berta had her laptop out, looking for jobs with a higher paying salary, while Johnny was sleeping next to her on the couch. Jessica arrived home from school.

"Hey! How did school go? Your grades came in the mail. Would you like to talk about it?" Miss Berta asked. "I failed everything." Jessica replied, as she walked upstairs disgusted. Miss Berta didn't make anything out of her behavior. She continued to work on her job applications. An hour and a half passed by, and Johnny woke up. He ran around the house in a hyper state, because he had eaten candy at preschool earlier in the day, while the other children played with the toys in the classroom. This allowed Johnny to take candy from the other children's lunchboxes.

The following day, Johnny kept laughing at Miss Berta. "Johnny boy, would you please stop laughing? I have a headache," she said. Johnny laughed and laughed. "Okay." He smiled. "No!" He squealed suddenly, bursting into laughter, until Miss Berta watched him run around the room uncontrollably. Johnny ignored Miss Berta's facial expressions. Many people found her scowl to be one of the scariest sights to see, but not for little Johnny. Little Johnny squealed aloud uncontrollably and laughing at her, "Hooray, hooray, and hooray," he yelled.

Upstairs, Jessica heard the commotion and shrieked, "Would you please shut up downstairs!" She belted, while Johnny the crying from Johnny persisted. Miss Berta continued to watch him run around the room. Jessica came downstairs to find out what was causing the noise. "What did you do to my baby brother?" She interrogated rudely. Little Johnny finally became exhausted from running around the room, and sat down on the floor.

"Look, we need to get down to the bottom of why he is so hyperactive," Miss Berta responded to Jessica.

Days passed, and Johnny's parents constantly gave him candy to stop him from crying. The candy made him run up and down the house with streamers. He laughed hysterically, while Miss Berta watched him run around the room wildly. As each day went by, Miss Berta became more and more agitated. Little Johnny made it into a comedic event. Each morning, his parents left him with bags of candy bags. He was the only one, who thought Miss Berta was funny. Anything she did made him laugh. He couldn't speak very well, because his parents never encouraged him. They never had the time nor interest to pay him much attention.

That night, Miss Berta finally settled the children to sleep. Little Johnny's fit earlier, had made it difficult for Miss Berta to focus. She fell into a deep sleep on the couch. Exhaustion overtook her and she began to dream.

In her dream, a middle aged, adult woman with a short bob haircut, lay in bed, while reading and drawing. As she lay there, preoccupied in her activities, two young women hurried inside the bedroom, giggling.

"Guess who's outside waiting for you?" The tall woman asked.

"Vous êtes folle!" The girl muttered, as she continued to draw images on paper.

"Would you stop with those fashion drawings, Will is outside!"

"Stop joking around," the young woman snapped.

"Berta, I'm serious," one of them responded. The young, fresh-faced girl was Miss Berta, who immediately leaped from her bed, to rummage through her closet, which was filled with clothes. Suddenly, Miss Berta awoke from her dream, as a middle-aged woman

Nick was in Central Park, with his Boy Scout friends. They were telling ghost stories. Each of them brought their sleeping bag to camp outside. Nick and his pals were always on adventures in the backyard. They spent their free time outside, and always hosted events in the tree house, where his father built for him, when he was younger. Nick was an amazing storyteller. He was a legend for telling scary stories to the Boy Scouts, who were afraid of his last werewolf story.

It was dark. The boys hadn't brought their flashlights to Central Park. Nick brought along his coolest toys, G.I. Joe action figures. The Boy Scouts envied him, because he had all the toys in the world. He also had one of the richest fathers in Manhattan. But he was never taught how to make a camp-fire, an important skill to obtain the badges for passing the Boy Scout requirement. His father was never around to teach him those kinds of things, although his father had been a Boy Scout also.

Mrs. Williamson spent time with the other mothers in the neighborhood, until it was time for her to go to another nightly function with her husband, Ted.

Miss Berta wasn't used to disorder. She was easily frustrated. The children never listened, and were constantly out of control. It was Tuesday night, and

Miss Berta could not take the chaos any longer. She wasn't getting any job offers, after constant attempts of applying to various magazine companies.

The children did their usual routine, while Miss Berta yelled at all three of them. "What on earth are you doing?" She shrieked. Jessica and Nick were shocked, while Little Johnny cried. Miss Berta firmly asked them to sit down. Johnny was being belligerent, so Miss Berta picked him up, and sat him down on the couch. She made her announcement quick and short, detailing her rules of conduct. The children were to inform her of their whereabouts throughout the day. They also had to show her their homework after they finished. Lastly, they would eat breakfast, lunch, and dinner at the same time, during the day.

Miss Berta was tough on the Williamson children. They did not like their new schedules. Jessica thought she was too big to be hanging around her siblings, let alone eating with them at the same time. She disapproved of the rules.

"Why do we have to do this?" She said.

"Because I said so," Miss Berta replied.

"What about me and Johnny?" Nick inquired.

"The same goes for the both of you," Miss Berta announced.

Jessica approached Miss Berta. "We know you're here to collect your paycheck, so just do that and leave us alone. I thought we were friends." Jessica declared.

Miss Berta felt insulted by Jessica's comments. Heather Tillings, Miss Berta's ex-employee from *Eloquent Fashion Magazine* popped into Miss Berta's head abruptly. She was reminded of their last conversation when Heather blamed her for the downfall of *Eloquent Fashion Magazine*. It reminded her, of whom she was.

Miss Berta's goal was to help Jessica and the children, who couldn't stand her. She didn't want to fail as a nanny, like she had at *Eloquent Fashion Magazine*. She wanted to change her domineering personality, and was aware that people kept their distance from her, because she was overpowering and demanding. Her goal was to contribute to society in a positive way, through the use of her newfound interpersonal skills.

Nick complained to his mother, every time she entered the house. He was like a reporter, giving his mother updates on Miss Berta's behavior.

"I don't like these rules she has Mom." Nick would say, and his mother would simply reply, "Just try them out."

This put Miss Berta in a bad state at times. Nick lied to his mother, insinuating that Miss Berta was breaking his toys. Miss Berta confronted him regarding these false allegations.

"Nick, why are you constantly complaining about someone breaking your turtle toys? I arrange them in order." Miss Berta declared.

Nick shrieked back at her, "Leave my turtles alone!"

Miss Berta decided to reveal to Mr. and Mrs. Williamson Jessica's close-call suspension from school. She cared deeply for Jessica's wellbeing and not only wanted her to succeed in life, but in school also. Miss Berta felt she would have to confront reality and tell the truth to the Williamson parents, in hope that it would make them a stronger family unit. Jessica was upset with Miss Berta for a full week, for exposing her secret. Miss Berta asked Jessica to watch her other siblings. "Watch your brothers!" She said, while she ran errands for Mr. and Mrs. Williamson, who were out on their usual excursions.

Miss Berta decided to call Heather Tillings the night before, to make amends with Jessica. Heather was now a full-time model. "Can you take her shopping today? I need to watch the other two." Miss Berta replied.

"I haven't been doing your style of fashion for months," Heather admitted.

"You couldn't forget. Once you're part of fashion, you never forget. You take it with you, no matter where you go. I have faith you won't let me down." Miss Berta confessed. Heather accepted the request, because Miss Berta's portfolio and letter of recommendation gave her a full-time modeling position at *Elle* magazine. The time spent apart from Miss Berta, also gave Heather time for reflection. It made her realize that she should forgive Miss Berta. Regardless of her differences, she became a high profile model because of Miss Berta's ambition for *Eloquent Fashion Magazine's* previous success.

Romero, her former photographer, was also hired at *Elle,* as the main photographer. Jessica was eavesdropping on the landline telephone, while Miss Berta was speaking to Heather. Jessica grew excited. She began to realize that fashion is life.

The following day, Heather rang the Williamson doorbell, while Miss Berta was in the living room. Jessica screamed from the balcony of the house. "Get the door! Can't you do anything?" Jessica reprimanded, while she stomped her feet as she walked downstairs, mad at Miss Berta. She opened the front door. "Oh my goodness," she gasped, immediately recognizing Heather as one of the high profile models in New York City. Heather smiled, as she stood outside on the front steps in jeans and a white shirt. "Hello, is Miss Berta here?" She asked. Jessica looked at Miss Berta, speechless. She let Heather inside the house. "It's for you," Jessica mumbled, feeling embarrassed for yelling. Miss Berta smiled and thanked Jessica for answering the door. Jessica had a bright look on her face. Miss Berta introduced Jessica to Heather.

"This is Heather. She used to work for me at *Eloquent Fashion Magazine* as a model. I asked her to take you shopping. She knows all there is to know about fashion." Miss Berta said smiling. Heather smiled back. Jessica didn't respond.

"You're going to spend the day with Heather." Miss Berta announced. Jessica ran upstairs to find her coolest punk, graffiti t-shirt. Jessica was impressed with Heather's clothing. She could not hold back her excitement.

Jessica arrived home with Heather later that evening. She said good-bye to Heather and thanked her. She closed the door behind her, while Miss Berta sat on the couch, reading. Johnny was asleep, while Jessica approached her. "I'm sorry I misbehaved." She said.

Miss Berta nodded. "I forgive you," she responded.

From that day on, things were cordial between Jessica and Miss Berta. Miss Berta told her stories about being Editor in Chief at *Eloquent Fashion Magazine*.

"Working as an Editor in Chief for a high profile magazine, was the highlight of my life." Miss Berta admitted.

"I can't believe you. You never said anything," Jessica said.

"That is in the past." Miss Berta replied.

Heather stopped by with her son occasionally, while Miss Berta gave her a lecture on the fashion industry. Heather used this time as an opportunity, to give Jessica some of her old clothes from *Eloquent Fashion Magazine*. Their conversations were brief, but meaningful,

"These are lovely." Jessica admitted, while Heather smiled, "They belong to you now. Take care of them, they are expensive clothes." Heather
said, while Jessica listened intently. "Do you think I should highlight
my hair?" Jessica would ask. Heather simply smiled. Jessica became enthralled with the fashion scene. She bought magazines, to research the
new fashion trends each month. Jessica knew the current fashion designers. Miss Berta took Jessica under her wing to help Jessica design her own
clothes.

Meanwhile, back at the house, Johnny and Nick played in their rooms
with their action toys, while Mrs. Williamson did yoga. Mr. Williamson was
at work and Miss Berta had initiated, that she would take Jessica shopping.
Mrs. Williamson agreed and stayed home with the two boys.

"My mom shops here," Jessica announced as they passed a small boutique called Cacique, which specialized in sixty-era dresses.

Jessica was overwhelmed with passion for style. One night after school,
Miss Berta bought Jessica a sewing machine. "Why did you leave *Eloquent
Fashion Magazine*? You were so talented!" Jessica inquired.

"I had no choice. The top fashion representatives didn't like the direction I was taking the photo shoot and my ideas for graffiti-style clothing,"
Miss Berta replied.

"I still think you're amazing," Jessica said. Miss Berta smiled, while she
glanced at Johnny, who was playing soccer with his imaginary friend, Bert.
Jessica looked at him too, and smiled.

Jessica faced Miss Berta with a look of anticipation on her face. "What
is it?" Miss Berta asked.

"However can you tell?" Jessica inquired.

"I just knew he had an imaginary friend," Miss Berta responded.

Jessica nodded. "Where are Mom and Dad?" she asked.

"Your father has a business function. Your mother went with him."

Jessica stood with her arms crossed and leaned against the kitchen counter. "Can you make my band's performance outfits for the Ovia Center? The
show is coming up." Jessica asked, changing the subject.

Miss Berta agreed to make the outfits for Jessica's band. It was one of
the band's biggest performances. It would be held at the Ovia Center, a huge
arena where many local concerts took place.

Drawing the band's ensemble was a challenge for Miss Berta. Jessica used her persuasive skills to get Miss Berta's to consent to the task.

"You have to go back to the fashion industry. You are wasting your talent here, but we are so happy you are here to stay, since *Eloquent Fashion Magazine* is out of business," Jessica mentioned.

Miss Berta was shocked. She listened intently to Jessica. "What do you know?" She asked.

"You're the most impressive woman in the entire globe in the fashion market," Jessica added.

"Stop it, child!" Miss Berta replied.

"But it is the truth. I know it is," Jessica responded.

"It was a long time ago," Miss Berta said.

"No it was not, people still speak of you and the magazine," Jessica said.

Miss Berta turned from Jessica's remarks, disgusted by past memories.

"I don't understand Miss Berta, you were the most respected woman in the fashion world. How is it possible that you feel this way?" Jessica said.

"It is none of your business Jessica. Let me be. Your clothes are ready, just let me be," Miss Berta replied.

It was the day of the concert, the crowd waited outside the Ovia Center, buying their tickets for the Knox Band performance. Upon entering to the arena, Jessica was the first to stand before the crowd in dim lights of red, blue, green, and yellow. The stage was decorated in a chessboard form. The band members wore black-and-white printed pants with long-sleeved shirts. The band members also wore brown cowboy boots. "Ladies and gentlemen, let me present to you our band, Knox." Jessica made the announcement, as the crowd of five thousand people went ballistic with cheers and applause. "One, two and three, hit it!" Jessica belted.

Andre and Zyrock started to play the music. The crowd continued to go wild. Zyrock pounded his drums in a fluid pace to Andre's smooth rhythmic bass. Jessica swayed her hips from side to side, as she sang to the crowd of people.

"Come to me. Come with me. You are so close. Yet, you are so far. I have lived. I have died. Come to me. Come with me, you are so close. Yet, you are so far. Come to me." Jessica sang.

Miss Berta promised Jessica that she would attend the show. She waited for her when the show ended, lights flashed from every direction of the stage. They blinded Miss Berta's eyes, but the time continued to pass with Knox fans taking pictures, wanting signed autographs. Miss Berta and Jessica arrived home at three o'clock in the morning. Mr. and Mrs. Williamson waited for them in the kitchen, with the lights dimmed.

"Where were you, why was my daughter out so late?" Mrs. Williamson demanded sternly.

Miss Berta fell silent, but Jessica interrupted. "Mom, do not yell at her. What did she do? Nothing," Jessica reprimanded her mother.

"Go to your room, child!" Mrs. Williamson responded.

"But, Mom—"

"Now!" Mrs. Williamson yelled. Jessica hurried upstairs. Mr. Williamson intervened, while Mrs. Williamson was ready to explode with anger. "Would you calm yourself, woman." Mr. Williamson intervened.

Mrs. Williamson crossed her arms and pouted, letting Mr. Williamson take over the interrogation. "Where were you both?" Mr. Williamson asked.

"Your daughter is in a rock band. I went to support her and bring her safely home," Miss Berta responded.

"Why didn't you tell us she had been living elsewhere, in an apartment with these band members?" Mr. Williamson interrogated.

Gasping, Miss Berta felt she had no choice but to speak the truth. "I wanted to support her dreams, she's very passionate about music and I didn't want to be responsible for crushing her dreams. I'm sorry, I lost track of the time, but I was clueless about the apartment." Miss Berta admitted.

"It shouldn't happen again. We are to be informed, concerning the events which takes place in our children's whereabouts," Mr. and Mrs. Williamson announced.

Miss Berta was shocked to discover that the Williamson parents were beginning to care for their children. She realized she was having a positive effect on them. Nick was a prime example. He became close to Miss Berta and trusted her.

The following week, Nick's Boy Scout friends stopped to speak to him. "Nick, you have to show us how to make campfires," a boy with brown hair said.

"I agree," a boy with blond hair had said. Meanwhile, Nick was in the backyard, creating campfires. The other Scouts were impressed at his improvement.

Tommy, a ten-year-old boy with long red hair, appeared. "Where did you learn that?" He asked.

"My nanny, Miss Berta," Nick replied and told the story of how Miss Berta helped him. "It all began with my usual complaining, and Miss Berta got sick and tired of it." Nick confessed, while the Boy Scouts gathered round. He explained to them that he had complained to Miss Berta about his inability to make campfires. He continued to tell the story.

"'All you had to do was ask,'" Miss Berta replied. "She gathered wood, twigs, dry leaves, small sticks, and branches, placed them in a circle of rocks. She picked up the sticks from the ground and began rubbing them together; and smoke began to appear. I was shocked. 'How did you learn that?' I asked her. "One of my models, who worked for me for a time, learned how to start campfires. It was part of one of the photo shoots for a summer issue for *Eloquent Fashion Magazine*," Miss Berta explained, as she walked off.

"Thank you, Miss Berta, I appreciate it, I responded. Miss Berta smiled to herself and went into the house. "Don't forget to put it out," she said.

Nick ended the story, and nodded his head while he stomped out the campfire with his boots. He was doing it as a demonstration as he told the story. The Boy Scouts gave him a round of applause for a great story.

Nick and Miss Berta became friends after she showed him how to make a campfire; Nick couldn't be happier.

Johnny also changed his attitude toward Miss Berta. She began taking candy away from his bedside table each morning, before he woke up. The first few days were chaotic; Johnny cried when she did this. One time, he even kicked Miss Berta in the leg, but she did nothing. Nevertheless, their relationship was improving with effort on her part.

Johnny went to Pebble Preschool, a private school for toddlers. These children were rambunctious. Sometimes, Miss Berta was overwhelmed, as the toddlers rushed into the preschool building. Their parents were relieved once they dropped off their children. At times, Miss Berta assisted the pre-school. She eased into the children's hearts. She would read the children friendly stories. She always read *The Little Red Riding Hood* to the preschoolers, which was the end-of-year school play.

Miss Rupert, Johnny's preschool teacher, invited Miss Berta to help design the costumes for the play. Miss Berta designs consisted of an urban theme, sticking to the story of *The Little Red Hood* plot. Miss Berta designed *The Little Red Riding Hood* costume to be capped in a red beret instead of a hooded cape, with red pants and jewelry stitched into the embroidery on the neckline. The black-and-red boots could be easily slipped on, once the costume was worn.

The day of Johnny's play; Nick, Jessica, and Miss Berta were Johnny's support system. On stage, a little girl named Rebecca was Little Red Hood. She was transformed in her costume. Johnny was in black and gray makeup, instead of the typical Wolf costume. The event was more of a fashion show than the actual telling of the story *The Little Red Riding Hood*.

Overall, the event was a success, except Johnny who expected his mother and father to attend the show. As Johnny recited his lines, he trembled with fear.

"Go, Johnny, you can do it." Nick began to clap. Johnny sulked on stage. He was looking for his parents and could not find them. Jessica clapped her hands together for support. The audience fell quiet, waiting for Johnny to continue his monologue. He could not continue and ran offstage into Miss Berta's arms, while she was seated in the front row. The audience clapped, out of respect. Miss Berta simply stood up and said to Nick and Jessica, while holding Johnny, "Let's go home." They exited the building.

At home, Jessica and Nick went to their bedrooms, while Miss Berta held Johnny.

"Is there something you want to tell me?" Miss Berta inquired softly, as she smiled.

"No." Johnny blurted out.

"Well can I make you some hot chocolate?" Miss Berta asked directly, while Johnny's spirits began to lighten with gratitude.

"Yes please," he responded.

"Good, then I'll read to you, your favorite bedtime story," Miss Berta replied. Johnny began to settle down, while Miss Berta received an important call from Bill Hoover, which interrupted Johnny's bedtime story. Johnny waited for Miss Berta, to pick up her cell phone in the hallway. She was invited to a long and tedious meeting, and agreed to meet with Bill Hoover. "Please call me tomorrow, Miss Berta instructed, as she hung up the cell phone. She entered Johnny's bedroom. "Now let's keep reading." Miss Berta said, as she resumed reading the bedtime story to Johnny.

The following day, Miss Berta was at home, while she received a second call from Bill Hoover. She picked up the line, "who is this?" She inquired.

"This is Bill Hoover. I am a business investor for television and print magazines. I would like to speak to Miss Berta London." The man answered.

"How may I help you, sir? How did you get my number?" Miss Berta inquired.

"Heather Tillings, an old associate of yours, made it my business to contact you. I was impressed with how highly she spoke of you. I would like to set up a formal meeting to discuss some important business. Please meet me at my office at Hoover Inc, located in Central Manhattan." The man hung up the phone.

The following day, Miss Berta entered the large Hoover Inc. building, and was greeted by receptionists dressed in business attire. She waited for Bill in the lobby on the thirty-fourth floor. He was preoccupied with flirting with one of his secretaries, who wore a mini-skirt, a white fluffy blouse, and pink lipstick.

"Mr. Bill Hoover, you have a client waiting for you," the lady announced.

Mr. Bill moved away from his secretary. "She's here?" He inquired.

"I've arranged everything for you today," the lady responded.

"Very good, Miranda," Mr. Bill replied, as he walked toward Miss Berta, who was seated in the lounge, reading an exercise magazine called *Fitness*. Mr. Bill opened the door into the lounge room. "Please, come inside, Miss London."

Miss Berta followed his instruction and closed the door behind her. "Take a seat," Bill indicated, as he showed Miss Berta a chair.

"Thank you," she said. Miss Berta slowly took a seat, as Mr. Bill watched her in awe.

"I'm honored to have you here, Miss London," Mr. Bill said.

"It's a pleasure to be here in your presence," Miss Berta responded.

"I've a proposal for you. One that will change your life," Mr. Bill informed her excitedly.

"Sir, I have yet to encounter such a proposal," Miss Berta admitted.

Mr. Bill placed a pack of documents before her. She took them, watching Bill intently. Both were overtaken by silence, Miss Berta took them and read each page carefully.

Contract:

I hereby give my authority to accept Bill Hoover's proposal, a family magazine, which is to set positive attributes for families. I give my promise and consent, as the new face and editor of this new business project, to honor and respect family values involving parents and their children. As Mr. Bill Hoover's business partner, it is my responsibility to disclose all information in regards to present and future business-related issues to the financier/business partner, who is also responsible for consorting present and future business relationships with the new face and editor of the upcoming business proposal. Both parties are in agreement to the following clauses:

CLAUSE 1:
All children/young adults between the ages of three to eighteen years must have parental consent to be featured in the upcoming magazine's business plan.

CLAUSE 2:
All parents have the right to any information in regard to their children. Principal requirements for this business proposal, the new name of company shall be called Miss Berta and the Family Magazine.

CLAUSE 3:
All constituents of this business proposal have the right to have a lawyer present, in regards to the signature consent of mutual agreements from all counterparts of this business proposal.

CLAUSE 4:

If parents feel a breach of contract has occurred, legal action will take place on all accounts. I hereby have read this business contract and I agree to all the terms. Signatures below shall make this contract binding. Please remember while also signing. This is a nondisclosure agreement between all parties involved.

Miss Berta finished reading the contract. She looked up at Bill. "Are you serious about this proposal, Bill? You are willing to finance a new magazine. And you would like me to take charge of it?" Miss Berta queried.

Mr. Bill nodded his head with approval. "Just as long as you bring up the ratings and keep them steady, bring that magic back," Bill announced.

"But children? My expertise is in the fashion industry," Miss Berta replied.

"The fashion industry for the young generation is a huge market, that should be tapped into. It has yet to be, and I think I am the first to tackle it," Mr. Bill concluded.

"I am in complete awe of this proposal, Bill!" she exclaimed.

Mr. Bill smiled, as Miss Berta picked up a pen from her handbag. She contemplated whether or not to sign the document. She placed the documents on her lap, and finally signed her signature. Mr. Bill picked up his own pen and signed his signature adjacent to Miss Berta's.

"Pleasure doing business with you, Miss Berta. I will make a photocopy of this for your records," he said, while he hit a button on his desk.

His secretary answered. "Yes sir?" She replied.

"Miranda, I need you to make a copy of a document and give a copy to Miss Berta."

"No problem, sir." Miranda walked in, quickly collected the contract from Bill, and returned with the copied version, which she handed to Miss Berta. Bill stood up to shake Miss Berta's hand and walk her to the exit.

Miss Berta was greatly missed by her old *Eloquent Fashion Magazine* fans. Yet as happy as she was, she was also sad that she had to leave the Williamson family.

It took three days before Miss Berta signed the contract. Early Monday morning, she stopped Mrs. Williamson on her way to yoga to break the news. "I wish to tell the children some important news, when they arrive home," Miss Berta announced.

"They are not going to take this lightly." Mrs. Williamson responded, while she grabbed her yoga mat, and walked out the door.

Later that afternoon, the children sat down on the living room couch, waiting for their parents. Mrs. Williamson entered the room and spoke. "Hi, children, Miss Berta has some news to tell us." She replied.

The children looked confused and tired. Johnny fell fast asleep. Miss Berta woke him up as she entered the room.

"Hi, children, I am glad I got the opportunity to be your nanny. You have definitely livened up my life in all sorts of ways, and I am saddened to leave you. I got hired to start a new magazine. The industry needs me," Miss Berta concluded.

There was a moment of silence. Mr. Williamson stood idle beside his wife. Jessica sprang up from her seat. "So you're just going leave, just like that?" Miss Berta tried to calm her down, but Jessica took off running upstairs. "Why bother becoming a nanny, when you don't even care for us?" Jessica cried.

"I do care for all of you, but I have been issued a once in a lifetime opportunity, that may never come again," Miss Berta responded. Meanwhile, Mrs. Williamson patted Nick on the shoulders, as he wept. "Who's going to show me cool stuff, so I can tell the rest of the Scouts?" Nick mumbled.

Miss Berta looked up at Mr. Williamson. "I am sure your father has many great stories to tell you," she replied.

Nick jumped up from his seat. "Yes, but his stories are boring, and he never has time for us." He took off running upstairs.

Mrs. Williamson picked up little Johnny, who was wiping away his tears. "Who's going to take candy from me, so I not laugh?" Johnny cried in his mother's arms.

Miss Berta was in tears. "I am so sorry." Miss Berta replied, while she gave in her final two weeks notice. She continued working with the Williamson family for the next upcoming two weeks. Mr. Williamson gave her the last paycheck for the remainder of the month. Miss Berta remained a friend of the family. She was included in the Williamson's family portrait, which came out two weeks later in the local New York City newspaper. The

Williamson family portrait was always featured in the paper. It had been a family tradition from Mr. Williamson's grandparents, who were considered high society at their era.

Miss Berta was about to leave at the time Jessica had calmed down.

"Can you do me one last favor before you leave?" Jessica inquired.

"Of course I can." Miss Berta replied.

"Can you come to my school and speak about your days as a fashion editor?" Jessica asked.

"I will be there on Monday next week," Miss Berta replied, tears streaming down her face.

It was Monday morning, Miss Berta was seated in the assembly hall near the teachers, who smiled and shook her hand with enthusiasm, as they took their seats. The assembly hall was filled with teenage students Principal Hunt stood before the crowd and podium.

"Welcome students, we have a very special guest, who has agreed to speak with you. Jessica Williamson arranged this for you, so you have her to thank. Will Jessica Williamson come to the podium." Principal Hunt announced.

The crowd of teenagers in the assembly clapped, while Jessica made her way to the podium, Miss Berta smiled at her. "Thank you Principal Hunt," Jessica said.

"Welcome my fellow students and staff!" Jessica said aloud. The crowd cheered, as they fell quiet. Jessica turned to face Miss Berta, who was seated behind her. "Miss Berta London, former editor of *Eloquent Fashion Magazine*, will you please stand up." The assembly of teenagers and teachers stood up to applaud her. Miss Berta did as she was instructed. She sat back down as the crowd returned to their seats, as the clapping subsided. "This woman with the vibrant red hat is a force to be reckoned with. She has been part of the fashion world for her entire life and has taken care of my brothers and me. I brought her here to speak with us." Jessica continued as the audience stood up, to give Miss Berta another round of applause. As the crowd settled, Jessica instructed, "Miss Berta London, please tell us your story. We all seek your inspiration."

Miss Berta stood up to take the podium, as the assembly went wild. She glanced at Jessica; a tear streamed down her face. "Thank you for that beloved introduction Jessica. Well, let's get started. As a child, I wanted to help children, to please my father. Needless to say, mothers can be controlling." Miss Berta giggled to herself, as the crowd giggled along with her. "To make a long story short, I was weaseled into the fashion world as a child, I wanted my mother to grow fond of me. My mother took me with her to all the runway shows around the city, and we traveled internationally when I was in high school. I was well acquainted with drawing designs and very well known in the fashion industry. My mother booked me several jobs for the top designers in the city. Once I graduated from high school, I went straight to work, and I was set. It took me years to switch careers. Although, I am not entirely in the fashion world anymore, I have served as a shopper, nanny and personal stylist. I have changed so much since *Eloquent Fashion Magazine* went out of business. Now, I'm actually stating a new magazine for your age group, which I am very excited about." The assembly went loud with cheer.

Miss Berta raised her arm up, to calm the noise. "I couldn't have done it without the Williamson family, and I thank them for that. My advice to you young people is to have your dream, keep your dream, and keep nurturing it till it comes true, that's what I did. Thank you, Glendale High School, for having me. Take care and good luck." Miss Berta concluded.

The entire assembly stood up to clap. Principal Hunt returned to the podium. "Thank you, Miss Berta London. Now, everyone, time to get to class," Principal Hunt instructed. Students began exiting the assembly, while Miss Berta shook the teachers' hands. She began to walk toward the exit of the hall and accidently bumped into a woman in a blue dress. "I'm sorry." Miss Berta said.

"Not a problem, great speech. It was very moving," the woman replied.

"Who are you?" Miss Berta inquired at this idle, mysterious woman.

"My name is Henrietta. I'm the substitute nurse at Glendale High School, just for today." The lady responded.

"That's great." Miss Berta replied sarcastically.

"Well, I wish my son could have heard your speech. He would have found you very inspiring," Henrietta responded.

"Well, doesn't he attend this school? What is his name?" Miss Berta asked.

"His name is A. J, and he doesn't attend this school," Henrietta replied, glad that Miss Berta was taking an interest in her.

Miss Berta's facial expression began to change. Miss Berta remembered the boy, who stalked Jessica's jam session in front of the Williamson's home garage. Miss Berta remembered the boy, and did not want to get too involved in the woman's business, "Well it was nice meeting you." Miss Berta replied. She walked away remembering that the boy had told her; that he didn't have a family.

Three months later, Miss Berta's debut magazine, *Miss Berta and the Family Magazine* was published. She had a diverse staff of new photographers and writers. Some were in the fashion arena, others were dancers; some were theater professionals, and some were athletes. Needless to say, all were graduates from college and were professionals in their fields. They each had something to offer the teenage demographic. The topics discussed in the magazine were question-and-answer sessions concerning homework and afterschool activities. Teenagers were invited on the set, for insights that would be featured in the magazine. Miss Berta recruited the children with help from the Williamsons. They maintained friendship with her.

The magazine had school fashion ideas, like school clothing, how to dress up or dress down your uniform, time management, passing exam tips and how to follow your passion by getting top grades.

The Williamson children received Miss Berta's first issue in the mail. It took a few days before Jessica picked up the mail from the mailbox, and flipped through it. She instantly saw the portrait of her family and the headline above it, *"Miss Berta and the Family Magazine."* She ran inside the house to show the entire family. "Look!" Jessica passed the magazine around the room. It was the same family portrait that appeared in the newspaper.

Meanwhile, the telephone rang. Mrs. Williamson picked up the telephone, it was Miss Berta on the line.

"I would like the children to come on an interview," Miss Berta said.

"It's Miss Berta! Children! She's inviting you to be part of her magazine." The Williamson children jumped in excitement.

The Williamson children were invited to speak with other children, who were also participants of the new magazine. Like the Williamson children, they too, faced challenges at home. Miss Berta helped the Williamson children tremendously. They developed into a stronger family. Mr. Williamson transitioned into a better father, one who made time for his children. He went on camping trips with Nick in the backyard. He went on hiking trips, and sometimes Johnny joined in on the outdoor adventures.

One day Mr. Williamson and his sons went on a fishing trip to Lake Erie, near Buffalo. They sat at the side of Lake Erie, with their fishing rods. Little Johnny had a toy fishing rod, of course, but that didn't stop him from feeling part of the group.

"So, Nick, how's school going so far, my son?" Mr. Williamson asked.

"Dad, you promised we wouldn't talk about school on this fishing trip," Nick protested.

"You are absolutely right, I promised to not discuss school," Mr. Williamson replied.

"Dad, look! I caught something—quick, come look." Little Johnny announced.

"Let's see," Mr. Williamson insisted as Little Johnny reeled in his toy fishing line. To their surprise, Little Johnny actually had caught a fish.

"It's a small goldfish," Mr. Williamson said.

"Good job, Johnny," Nick congratulated. Nick and Mr. Williamson wrapped up the goldfish in a clear bag with collected water from the lake, because it was time to go.

Mrs. Williamson also developed a close bond with Jessica. They were seated at a table outside at a small restaurant called Lule. The sun was shining, while Mrs. Williamson was in her yoga attire. She picked Jessica up from school, to spend some quality time with her. As they both waited for their food, Mrs. Williamson said, "Do you want to tell me about your day?"

Jessica smiled. "Well, my grades have improved." Jessica took out her most recent progress report." She showed them to her mother.

Mrs. Williamson smiled with enthusiasm. "Congratulations, I am proud of you," she said encouragingly. "We both deserve to go shopping for this." Mrs. Williamson said to her daughter.

7

THE OTHER SIDE OF TOWN

Miss Berta entered her extravagant office, located in the heart of New York City. The high-rise building on Madison Avenue had fifty-four floors. The scenic view of tall, tightly packed buildings were a beautiful sight, from where she stood. She peered out the window; the people down below looked miniscule, like ants. Miss Berta stood at her window a changed woman. She transformed from a careless, iron heart, to a soft, kind and gentle person.

Someone knocked at her office door. It was Leticia Benet, Miss Berta's assistant editor and personal secretary. She stood in the doorway.

"Leticia, what brings you in here?" Miss Berta asked.

"We have another atrocious story to feature in the magazine," Leticia announced.

Miss Berta smiled. "Nothing I can't handle, I always get the essence of the story in the interviews. What is it? Is it a disrespectful son, daughter? Do tell me?" Said Miss Berta.

"Well, let's just say this one is worse, from what I gather. It'll be a challenge to solve," Leticia responded.

Miss Berta paced up and down her office. The files were in Miss Berta's file cabinet, organized in chronological order from A-Z. She folded her arms and listened. Leticia took out a blue-covered folder labeled, The Johnsons. She took the folder from the nearby file cabinet. The folder Leticia held in her hand contained a printed newspaper article, which posted in the newspaper.

"A child who may be taken into foster custody," Leticia announced.

"Why do people treat their children in such a manner? What on earth?" Miss Berta said, her voice full of anger.

"The family is experiencing hardship; the father lost his job at the post office. He ran away from the family to pursue his music. He was the sole breadwinner," Leticia said with frustration. She sat back in the large armchair in the office, after she recounted the information pertaining to the article.

"I'm going to visit the Johnson family, to see what I can do." Miss Berta announced.

"Um...I don't think you should go out there Miss Berta," Leticia responded. Miss Berta's eyes widened, shocked at Leticia's boldness.

"Of course I'm going." Miss Berta replied.

It was a Wednesday afternoon. Miss Berta planned to leave the office at four o'clock to get a start on the drive to Brooklyn. At four o'clock on the dot, Miss Berta took off her heels and reached for her comfortable brown flat shoes. She swirled in her office chair and grabbed her car keys, the Johnson file, and a red apple that lay on her desk. Lastly, she snatched her polka-dot purse.

Miss Berta's employees were chatting among themselves, various conversations concerning what they were having for dinner, or what they were going to feed their house pets. It was not a terribly busy time of day at the magazine. Miss Berta walked past her talking employees. They wished her a safe journey. Most women in the office changed into their flats at this time of day, especially when Miss Berta wasn't around. The men loosened their ties. This was free time for the office. The entire office could relax; Miss Berta was on a new assignment. She made her way toward the elevator. Meanwhile, Leticia stopped her. "Miss Berta! Don't do it!" Leticia called. Miss Berta turned round rapidly. "What are you talking about?" She replied.

"You're going to Brooklyn to interview that family?" Replied Leticia. Miss Berta hesitated before responding. "So what if I am? This is my J-O-B Leticia. I signed on to do this magazine. As editor in chief, I will conduct the interview, so we can feature it in the new magazine. Be a good secretary and get me my coat. It's on my chair. " Miss Berta demanded.

Without another word, Leticia turned away and did as she was told. The employees stared with anticipation, witnessing an argument between the two.

"Get back to work!" Miss Berta snapped at her employees. Leticia came back from her office, and handed Miss Berta her brown coat. She got into the elevator and exited out the parking lot. She was on the ground floor. She got into her BMW convertible, and adjusted her seat. She turned on a country western station as she drove off. Miss Berta acquired this luxurious car, due to the pay advance she received from Bill Hoover. Bill Hoover wrote her a big grant for the first release of *Miss Berta and the Family Magazine*, which featured the Williamson children. It was a big success. The release of the first issue sold three million copies nationwide. It featured an article with Miss Berta as nanny, and the Williamson children speaking about Miss Berta's role in their lives. Miss Berta carried the first issue of *Miss Berta and the Family Magazine* in the front seat of her car. The front cover featured a photograph of the Williamson children, with Miss Berta in a vibrant red hat and a black chic suit, seated in white chair. The Williamson children stood next her, with their hands on her shoulder. The text on the photo read, "She's not only a nanny, but a mentor, stylist and GREAT FRIEND! Miss Berta glanced at the magazine and smiled. It wasn't long before her BlackBerry rang, she responded through her Bluetooth. "What is it, Leticia?"

"Be careful!" Leticia ventured timidly, before Miss Berta could say another word. Leticia hung up the phone. Miss Berta clicked the end-call button on the phone, while she was in the car. She was on her way to Brooklyn. It took forty-five minutes to get to the exit. As she drove toward the exit, she noticed the difference in scenery. The buildings on this part of town were run-down and spray-painted with graffiti. The houses were slanted and the stench was badly odorous, it was awful. Miss Berta rolled up her windows. She scrunched her face tightly to hold in her breath, and to prevent herself from breathing in the stench. She switched to a different station, which played classical music; to ease her worried thoughts.

Miss Berta finally reached her destination. The downtown people of Brooklyn were dressed differently. Many of them wore hats, which were turned backward, and pants that were baggy. People hung around the corner stores, talking to one another. Miss Berta was bewildered and did not know if she had the right directions to the Johnsons' home. She looked around cautiously, looking for someone she could ask for directions. She spotted an older man wearing glasses, using a cane, barely able to walk. She slowed down the car as, he was walking up the sidewalk, which was deteriorated and crumbling.

"Excuse me sir, do you know where the Johnsons live? I was told that there is only one family with that name, who lives on this block?" Miss Berta asked.

"Get back!" The man shouted, waving his cane at her.

"Sir, I just want to know where the Johnsons live," Miss Berta replied. He cooled off his temper, and pointed to a small flat home ahead of him. It was a run-down brick home. The side of the house had cracks in it, and seemed like it would not be able to withstand a snowstorm.

"Thank you sir," Miss Berta said to the man. She parked her car outside the house's driveway. As she got out of the car, she could feel the neighborhood eyes peering down her back. The front door had scratches through it. She opened it halfway and knocked, while she peeked her head inside; a slim woman with high cheekbones yelled at a tall teenage boy. Miss Berta served as an eyewitness, to the woman screaming at her son.

"You useless piece of crap!" The woman reprimanded the young boy.

"Mom I'm sorry, I forgot to pay the bill!"

The woman scolded her son. Out of nervousness, Miss Berta stood at the door.

"I'm not done with you yet!"

The woman's eyes bulged with anticipation. "Yes?" She said with a look of panic in her eyes, while she glared at Miss Berta. Miss Berta tried to control her gasping. She placed her hand on her chest and began breathing fiercely. "I was worried about..." Miss Berta hesitated.

"It's none of your business lady!" The woman slammed the door in Miss Berta's face. Miss Berta knocked on the door again. The woman angrily swung the door open.

"What is your problem?" The woman asked. Miss Berta smiled, recognizing the same woman she had encountered at Jessica's school. Miss Berta offered her hand for the woman to shake, but the woman declined. Miss Berta tried to introduce herself, stumbling over the slippery porch. "I am Miss Berta London." She hesitated. "I am a magazine editor at *Miss Berta and the Family Magazine*. Is it possible that I speak with you?" Miss Berta inquired. The woman slammed the front door in Miss Berta's face again.

8

THE JOHNSON FAMILY

The Johnson family consisted of a single mother and son AJ, a boy widely respected by his teachers at school, because so much was demanded of him at home. He was in his senior year, so it was crunch time for him to take the SAT examination.

AJ was a decent, respectful boy. He respected women highly and could not find it in his heart to tell a woman the word *no*. Although he had a girlfriend for six months, he did have a controlling personality, and was critical of anyone who fell short of his standards. He took this relationship seriously. Ariana was a serious girl, one who planned to study child psychology in college. AJ wanted to pursue a business degree. They both had a common goal, however, they wanted to leave the neighborhood, where they grew up. Ariana cared about what her friends thought of AJ, they described him as obnoxious and opinionated, so Ariana broke off the relationship. She avoided him at school, the distance between them enabled him to put the past behind him, and focus on school and his part-time job.

AJ struggled every day. He had no car and had to commute to and from school every day on the subway. His mother couldn't help him like she wanted, because she barely had enough money to pay the rent. Growing up, AJ was aware that his responsibilities were to take care of his mother, do his homework, and make sure he didn't miss one day at his current job at the restaurant.

AJ was a member of the kitchen staff at Starr Restaurant. The job gave him peace of mind; he didn't mind washing dishes or people insulting at him at work, he was used to it.

Benjamin Johnson, his father, left him and his mother when AJ was three years old, to pursue his music career. His mother tried to stop him, telling him not to go, because she loved Benjamin. She felt it was useless to keep him from going. In the end, she believed he would have hated her if she did not allow him to go.

Benjamin traveled the world, he performed in restaurants overseas, which was how he made his income. Henrietta, AJ's mother, called him from time to time. At first, he responded to the phone calls and the relationship stayed afloat for six months, until Benjamin stopped responding to her calls. This was a huge setback for Henrietta. The divorce papers arrived a year later. Henrietta didn't bother fighting it. She looked at the situation realistically. Benjamin was nowhere to be found, so all she did was sign the papers and send them back to Benjamin, so he signed his part. Once she received the signed copies from Benjamin, she sent them to the court for the divorce process to be completed.

The divorce finalized, it was a traumatic event in AJ's and Henrietta's lives. Fourteen years later, AJ, seventeen, had a lot of responsibilities on his shoulders. In the mornings before he went to school, he would buy groceries for the house. His list consisted of a loaf of bread, chicken, milk, and orange juice. Shopping was fun for AJ. Sometimes he used the remaining change on small treats for himself, candy or chips, other times it was chocolate milk. The grocery store was a place he loved. He enjoyed watching shoppers, trying to get into their world and figure out what life was like for them. It was a way for him to escape from his own reality.

Henrietta was hard on AJ. She did the best she could to raise him properly, considering she was a single mother. Her responsibilities were double those of the average mother; she had to be both mother and father. Henrietta was a nurse and often worked overtime. Her free time was limited, and she took all her anger and frustrations out on AJ. Once, when he was nine years old, his mother came home and smacked him across the face because she had a rough day. Her boss Timothy cut her hours for being late, after she dropped AJ off at school. AJ learned that he had to be independent and fast;

he had to take the bus and subway on his own every morning, and every afternoon. His mother lost the car because of her failed payments.

Miss Berta left the Johnson home, after the door was slammed in her face for the second time. She became frustrated at the situation, regretting that she didn't inform the Johnsons' she would visit. She realized that this task was going to be a difficult one to tackle. Miss Berta went home that night, contemplating how to handle the case. She put her kettle on the stove to boil and in less than five minutes, poured her tea. Soon afterward, the telephone rang. She put down her tea and walked over to answer it.

"Hello?" She murmured, exhausted.

"So how did it go?" Leticia inquired on the other line.

"Hello Leticia," Miss Berta responded.

"So you went, after I warned you?" Leticia said smugly.

"Yes, I did," Miss Berta replied sternly.

Leticia cautioned Miss Berta. She feared the outcome of getting involved in the Johnsons' case. It was rumored by the town, that the family was abnormal.

Nevertheless, it was all going in one ear and out the other with Miss Berta. She felt it was her calling in life to help the Johnson family. She had a long talk with Leticia that night. Their talk broke out into an argument.

"How dare you Leticia!" Snarled Miss Berta.

"Berta, it's dangerous for the magazine!" Leticia proclaimed.

"What are you talking about?" Miss Berta responded.

"Henrietta, is that nurse you met at Glendale High School? What if she doesn't support the magazine? What if she doesn't like if we feature her personal life in the magazine? She may speak ill of the magazine. It has been rumored, that the family is abnormal." Leticia continued on and on, while Miss Berta waited for her to settle down. Once their temperaments calmed, the conversation turned into an awkward silence. It was the first time Leticia and Miss Berta argued severely. Each individual highly respected the other, although Miss Berta was never married and Leticia was, she constantly gave Leticia advice on her personal relationships. Leticia had a one-year-old daughter, Savannah, who stopped by the magazine often, brought by Leticia's husband. Leticia's husband, Rick, was a relaxed man with a clean-shaven haircut. He was slim and debonair, his smile big and bright. He was a musician and a flirty one at that. Leticia didn't mind these attributes because she knew where his heart was. Nevertheless, it was a constant battle to fight for his attention. Miss Berta was always her marriage counselor.

The days rolled by since the argument between Leticia and Miss Berta. They passed each other at the office and greeted each other with a sly good morning and good afternoon. The greeting wasn't sincere from either end.

It was a rainy day. Miss Berta attempted to call the Johnsons, but there was no response. She walked into her office and closed the door behind her. Her office was filled with bright, extravagant colors. She adored yellow, lime green, baby blue, and orange. There was something about these colors that gave the impression that she was ostentatious. The colors were a reflection of her style. Miss Berta's past history with the Williamsons made her accept bright colors. Black, white, and red were no longer part of her personality. She was no longer sinister. The children made her fall for vibrant colorful colors. People were no longer intimidated to approach her.

The Williamsons were unified as a family. They did well as a strong, supportive family unit. From time to time, Miss Berta received mail from the family, who kept her informed of their current situation. Jessica was now nineteen, in her freshman year of college, and doing quite well on the tennis team. Nick was in high school, making a huge impression with his inventions in the science realm. Last but not least, Johnny was just falling in love with school. He was quite popular.

Miss Berta sat in her office, doodling on one of her notebooks regarding the Johnson case. She read the entire Johnson file on her office desk, which gave her insight into the family dynamic. She made a list of reasons to pursue the Johnson case versus the reasons not to. The pros were to help AJ develop his self-esteem, help the family become unified, help him go off to college and get an internship, where he can explore his horizons beyond his hometown. The cons displayed: The Johnson family may consider Miss Berta a conceited individual. The pros outweighed the cons and this gave Miss Berta the incentive to pursue the Johnson case.

9

MEET MY STEPFATHER LUCAS

The first image that appeared was a street sign reading Brooklyn. It was nerve-wracking because there wasn't a car in sight. Miss Berta was the exception; she got out of her car, and recognized the front steps of the Johnsons' home. Miss Berta approached the door and pushed it slightly open. She didn't go in. Instead, she stood there, pondering to go in or not. A loud boom was heard through the silence.

Miss Berta tripped into a dark room. It was the exact location she remembered AJ's mother yelling at him the previous day. A feeling of wonder overtook her. She stumbled to her feet out of fear and nervous energy, and got up to see who had pushed her with brutal force. No one was behind her. The air was brutally cold and miserable. Miss Berta began breathing heavily, fear surrounding her entire body. It was the second time she peered over her right shoulder, to get a glimpse of the potential suspect. The room was dark and hostile, and nobody appeared, except a slender, manly figure, which appeared in front of her. She couldn't make out his features, which were haunting her. Squinting her eyes to get a better look, she instantaneously recognized AJ. His head was down, while he stood there in his Nike sneakers and a striped black-and-brown hooded sweatshirt. She couldn't make out the expression on his face.

"Who goes there?" Miss Berta ventured, just to get a conversation going. AJ reached out his bloody arm to grab her.

"Ah!" Miss Berta squealed, waking up in her bed. It took a good minute, to come to the realization that it had all been a dream. Slightly sluggish, Miss Berta got up and looked at the cuckoo clock on her wall. It was 10:00 a.m.

Leticia had stopped by Miss Berta's home, to have a discussion about the disagreement the night before. After she left, Miss Berta was alone with no one to talk to about her dream. She gathered her things to prepare for the office. In one hand, she had her big black leather purse, into which she stuffed her thirteen-inch laptop, various documents, the Johnsons' file, her agenda book, and her car keys. Once she gathered all her things, she headed for the front door. She closed the door behind her because she was already late for work.

Upon her arrival at the office, and clearing her office workspace, she made the decision that she was not going back to work until she interviewed the Johnsons and became part of their lives, so she could obtain her next big story for the magazine. Miss Berta was convinced that it was her duty to help the Johnsons, especially AJ. The dream she had the previous night had been very strange. No one could tell her otherwise. It wasn't her fate, and deep down she believed she could help the Johnson family, and that she was the person for the job. With her background in education and previous nanny experience, she believed it to be possible.

Later that night, Miss Berta made an attempt to call the Johnsons. It took a few minutes for the phone to be answered. AJ just returned home from his job Starr Restaurant. His day was long and he was not in a good mood. It was Tuesday, and that meant he had to clean bathrooms. Not a fun job, but he had to help his mother pay the rent while he still lived with her.

Henrietta was out with Lucas, her new boyfriend. They usually ran errands around their neighborhood, while AJ had chores to do at home. Henrietta had been dating a man who was not the friendliest type. He was vicious, with a dogmatic personality. Henrietta was unable to grasp the concept of what it meant to truly love someone or be loved by someone. Her goal was to encourage him to be a better person and change as an individual. Henrietta believed Lucas would change and become a better person. Blinded by loneliness, she was unable to see this man in a bad light.

On the contrary, AJ thought of him as an opportunist. After her ex-husband left her, Henrietta never was the same. It never crossed her mind that she would end up divorced.

Lucas, on the other hand, never was married, and was always in and out of relationships. He lived his life dating multiple women at the same time, toying with their emotions. He dated different girls each day of the week. Nevertheless, since he met Henrietta, he stuck close to her like glue. She was easy to manage and control. He dumped other women he dated, because he got fed up with them and was unable to control or benefit from them financially.

If AJ wasn't arguing with his mother, he got into arguments with Lucas. These arguments were frequent and sometimes ended badly. AJ usually got a black eye from Lucas, while his mother never helped the situation. She blamed him for starting the drama. Although Lucas was the sole instigator. "Serves you right, if you only listened. Your pigheadedness will get you nowhere," Henrietta would yell at AJ.

Lucas was a husky man; one punch from him meant you were out for the count. There were countless times AJ fell unconscious because he was used as a punching bag.

Last Christmas, Henrietta discovered that Lucas stole her money. He cleared out her bank account, and she was unable to buy food—or anything else, for that matter—for an entire week. To top it all off, Lucas was out of sight and nowhere to be found. He reappeared at the Johnson home when all the money ran out. AJ warned his mother that Lucas might encounter problems with the law, but she never took anything AJ said too seriously. She was in love with Lucas, it didn't matter what he did. She always found it extremely hard to think he would get into too much trouble. Henrietta experienced physical abuse and emotional abuse from Lucas. She was in love with him, but also terrified to erupt the volcano of anger that was hidden deep in his personality.

Henrietta wore her blue nurse uniform and black leather shoes, the ones that she had for quite some time. She worked late nights, and sometimes sacrificed not going shopping for herself.

AJ was asleep. Meanwhile, Henrietta dressed for work, the phone rang.

"AJ, would you get that, darn it!" his mother called angrily.

Lucas was asleep, while he lay in bed with his mouth dripping with spit. "It's about time you got that lazy boy to do something around here!" Lucas interrupted, as he abruptly awoke from his sleep.

AJ got up slowly and dragged himself to the kitchen. "Yes?" He answered the telephone groggily, still in a daze.

"Hello is this AJ?" The voice responded.

"Yes, how do you know my name?" AJ responded.

"Let's just say we have been interested in your background AJ. We want to help you," replied the voice on the other line.

"What are you talking about?" AJ replied in haste.

Overhearing the telephone conversation, Henrietta became annoyed. "I am getting tired of people calling, like we have money for this telephone bill! Who are you talking to?" Henrietta barked at AJ angrily.

Henrietta grabbed the phone from AJ. "Hello, who is this?" she snapped.

"Oh, hi, you must be Henrietta." The voice said.

"You don't call my house to interrogate my son, saying you must be Henrietta. I don't know you! We aren't friends!" Henrietta said.

"Well I'm sorry, let me introduce myself. My name is Leticia, and I am Miss Berta London's secretary from *Miss Berta and the Family Magazine*," Leticia replied.

"Who?" Henrietta responded. "Look, thank you, but we do not need your charity cases. I can take care of my family." Henrietta slammed the phone down. On the verge of explosion, she turned to AJ, pointing in his face. "Do not answer one of their calls ever again! I am going to work!" Henrietta said, as she left the house in a furious state. Out of anger, she slammed the door behind her.

AJ peeked through the kitchen window, ashamed of himself. Outside, his mother waited at the bus stop. She had her arms crossed, while glancing at her watch. It wasn't long until the bus appeared, while she got on the bus.

It was a typical day. Lucas was out of the house, wasting Henrietta's money, which he stole. His mother was at work. Immediately after they both left AJ, who went to the telephone and dialed the memorized number, that Leticia had given him during their last private telephone discussion. He breathed heavily, as he dialed the numbers. "Hello, *Miss Berta and the*

Family Magazine, Leticia here to assist you," Leticia responded in a professional manner, as she picked up the telephone.

"Hey, it's AJ. We had a conversation earlier this morning," AJ replied. "Hi, AJ! I'll transfer you to Miss Berta," Leticia responded.

10

MISS BERTA INTRODUCES HERSELF

AJ was on the telephone. Moments later, the telephone was answered. Miss Berta was enthusiastic. It took her a moment to calm down.

"Hello AJ. Here at *Miss Berta and the Family Magazine*, we are in high spirits to hear back from you. I would like to set up an appointment with you, if that's okay?" Miss Berta announced in an elegant manner.

AJ hesitated. "Meet me tomorrow. Do you remember the address?" AJ murmured.

"Definitely, we have it in your file," Miss Berta replied.

"Okay good. Well, see you tomorrow, three o'clock should be a good time," AJ responded.

"Wait! What made your mother change her mind?" Miss Berta inquired.

"She realized we needed help," AJ announced.

"I'm glad she came around. Well, see you tomorrow," Miss Berta replied.

AJ put the phone down and took a deep breath. Lucas appeared in the doorway. His presence startled AJ. "What were you doing?" Harassed Lucas.

"Nothing," AJ replied as he lowered his head. AJ walked away with a scowl on his face. He went to his bedroom and closed the door.

The following afternoon, it rained with heavy thunderstorms. AJ's mother was frying eggs on the hot stove. She popped some bread in the toaster, and poured the remainder of orange juice into a glass. She wrapped the remaining food in plastic wrap, and headed out the door. It wasn't long until Lucas was dressed in his construction uniform, and followed her out of the front door.

The doorbell rang, AJ felt nervous. He slowly and patiently walked over and opened the front door. Miss Berta London stood outside, looking poised and professional.

AJ smiled at the sight of her. "Hopefully you didn't have trouble finding the place? From where you may live, it must have been far," AJ inquired.

"The distance was okay," Miss Berta replied patiently, while AJ let her into the house.

"Well, you can have a seat here." AJ directed Miss Berta, as he escorted her to one of the seats at the kitchen table. She placed her briefcase down beside the chair and smiled. "So, let's get down to business. AJ. I am here to help you. At *Miss Berta and the Family Magazine,* our main job is to interview families, work with them on their style, unify them, and feature them in *Miss Berta and the Family Magazine.* Each issue we change up of course."

AJ was overwhelmed by the information. He did not know where to start. He sat down, and took a deep breath.

Miss Berta waited for him to regain composure. Secretly, she wanted him to do most of the talking. It was a typical strategy of hers.

AJ felt awkward and did not know where to begin. He sat in the kitchen, placing his attention on a picture of Lucas, one that his mother had on the refrigerator. The moment he laid eyes on the photograph, he began babbling. He started explaining to Miss Berta the way he grew up and the reasons his biological father left them. He explained that his father abandoned his mother not long after his birth, because he wanted to pursue his dreams of becoming a well-respected saxophone player. AJ described the excruciating pain he endured each night, hearing his mother's tears from the constant fights she had with Lucas. "It's a feeling like you were born a mistake. That's one of the worst feelings to have; the feeling of not being wanted or feeling less important," AJ concluded.

Miss Berta listened closely to every word, on the verge of tears. She never heard a story quite like this in her entire life. She remembered the Williamsons' scenario, but this was different. This case left her in a state of misunderstanding. She didn't say a word, she took it all in, and it was a heavy load to absorb from a teenage boy, he was well spoken despite his circumstances.

"Your past memories are unbelievably tragic." She added, while she rummaged through her briefcase, with aggressive speed to retrieve her laptop. At this point, AJ was in a state of awe. His eyes were fixed on the computer Miss Berta took out of her briefcase. His jaw dropped. "Is that a Sconzy notebook?" He asked.

"It sure is," Miss Berta replied. "I'll tell you what. You get into college with a 3.0 GPA, and I will buy you one," Miss Berta proclaimed. AJ was still in disbelief. "I'm serious. You help me and I will help you," Miss Berta replied, while AJ stared at her in disbelief. "I'm serious," Miss Berta announced, as she explained her expectations. She declared her willingness to be his mentor, to get him through high school. In return, he had to be willing to quit his current job, at least until graduation.

"I'll quit my job first thing, but not right now. I have to help my mother with the bills at home," AJ replied. Miss Berta took his word for it, and that was the end of the conversation. She went through her written plans, the ones she prepped for AJ the night before, and handed him his weekly schedule. It had things he had to accomplish by the end of each week. It was prepped in a binder and was also indexed.

"So, what are your goals? AJ. What do you want to achieve? I am curious to know?" Miss Berta inquired.

AJ thought long and hard at the questions. "All I know is that I want to get away from here. I want to get away from Lucas, and I want my mother to get away too. I want to help her get away. We need change in our lives. I don't know what kind of change, but we need positive change. I just don't know how to go about it."

"Well, I can help you come up with a strategy," Miss Berta replied.

"I do a lot of reading about art and history and it would be nice to travel far from here, like to Europe or something. Getting an internship abroad would be ideal. My goal is to go to college, graduate and help my mother" AJ replied enthusiastically.

"Well, your number one priority should be your studies. I want you to have a planner and write out your goals and accomplishments, and think of different strategies; that will allow you to achieve them. Write a timetable for yourself." Miss Berta replied, as she took out her personal timetable.

Miss Berta left him with a story, detailing her days in high school as a teenager. To her credit, she belicved this story would inspire AJ, and show him how much they were alike growing up. Her parents were always on promenading around town, just like his.

11

THE PIN UP SOCIETY COMPETITION

Miss Berta closed her eyes, while AJ sat listening with anticipation. They sat at Henrietta's kitchen table, while Lucas and Henrietta were out for the day. "I remember the competition like it was yesterday. Ten mothers altogether, had enrolled their daughters into "The Pin-Up Society Competition." It was a competition for that generation. I was eighteen at the time, and my mother had gone abroad to participate in some European fashion show. It was the night before the event; the storm outside my bedroom window was horrendous. Lightning struck the ground. Meanwhile, I heard my mother and father arguing in the next room.

"Don't you see and hear the storm outside?" My father said to my mother.

"You are not going to stop me. I am going," my mother proclaimed. My father was quiet and slammed the door behind him. I could hear footsteps outside my bedroom door. I heard taps at the door to my bedroom. "Yes, Father," I said.

"Hello, dear, are you awake?" My father asked, as I was finishing the designs for my dresses and coats." Miss Berta continued.

Meanwhile, AJ interrupted Miss Berta's storytelling. "So you were a designer before you became a nanny?" AJ inquired.

"Yes AJ, but stop interrupting. Allow me to finish." Miss Berta replied.

"All right." AJ responded.

"All right, back to the story, like I was saying; he simply saw me drawing, finishing the sketches to my designs, while he looked at me in amusement. "What on earth have you done with the coat I brought you?" My father proclaimed. It was the coat he brought back for me from London, where my parents had gone for their anniversary. I had turned that coat into a long patterned, bright yellow and green gown, quite unusual for that era. Whenever I wore the coat, my father simply laughed. "What do you think your mother would say?" He asked.

"My mother entered the room just at that moment. "Berta, what on earth have you done with your coat?" She asked.

"I'm going to enter it into "The Pin-Up Society Competition," I said fiercely.

"She simply gazed at me. "Absolutely not," Mother said to me. My father left the room in angst at that point. Meanwhile, my mother continued to scold me. "You're going to have to start all over. That is hideous." She replied. I simply turned my face to ignore her. "Well, I leave tomorrow. I just wanted to wish you good luck. It is your duty to win, make you proud," she said. She gave me a hug and a kiss on the forehead. She exited my room and there I was, alone once again.

"The following day, mother was running up the staircase. 'Winston, are my bags at the door? Winston, are you ready to take me to the airport?' Mother said aloud.

"Of course," Winston, our butler responded, as he hastened down the stairway, struggling with four suitcases. My father waited impatiently while my mother finally descended down the stairwell fully dressed in a large, burgundy trench coat. She looked flawless and was ready for *Les Femmes European,* a European fashion competition in France.

"My mother approached my father and gave him a long good-bye kiss. Winston was in the car. He waved at me while my mother entered the car. My father was outside, standing with his briefcase. He looked up at me and waved as he got into his Volkswagen. I was in tears that I would be entering this competition with no support from my parents.

Winston waited for me outside the car, while I collected the ten dresses, which I designed previous nights before. He opened the white door to the

Bentley. As I got outside the car, I walked towards "The Pin Up Society Competition." As I was walking, I saw people moved about the city in Central Park. New York City was busy, as usual. The competition was held at the front of the Bethesda Terrace and fountain. The fountain itself depicted a female angel. I could see my competitors, ten girls stood with their mannequins, which they had dressed in their designs. I was running slightly late. The competitors were ready with their displays. Meanwhile, the judges were preparing themselves. I quickly unlocked my suitcase and unpacked my ensembles, to display on my mannequins: beige, green, brown, black, violet, yellow, pink, and red outfits. I noticed Miss Whitmore, my rival. Her mother had been my mother's rival when they were growing up, but luckily my mother was always one step ahead of hers.

As I was ready to start the competition, the judges passed the first contestant. She stood before the three judges, dressed in a straw hat and a long beige skirt and white blouse. Her ensembles revealed the same design she wore. The two women walked around her mannequins, as the male judge took notes on a notepad. None of them spoke a word. The second contestant wore the same plain beige dress, as the first contestant. Contestant number three, was Miss Whitmore, she was quite interesting. She designed pant-and blouse ensembles. The judges were impressed with her. Contestants four, five, six, seven, eight, and nine were similar to contestants one and two. They used dull colors for the designs of the dresses. I was contestant number ten. My mannequins were in a line of ten, and displayed my ensembles. The female judges looked at all of them; the male judge simply stood before my mannequin, who was dressed in bright, vibrant red top hat. The trench coat matched. All three judges took at least five extra seconds to examine the piece. One of them spoke to me, which was a shock.

"Interesting ensemble," he said.

"Thank you," I replied.

"'What is your name?' He asked.

"Berta London," I replied. The two female judges smiled at me. I could feel the glare from the other contestants, especially Miss Whitmore, who watched me. Her eyes pierced mine, and I could sense she was envious. Meanwhile, the judges walked back to their table. All of the contestants were nervous. We simply waited for the judges to organize themselves. I stood idle, while I saw parents cheering for their children. My parents were tending to their personal affairs, and this made me sad. I felt alone. The other parents were there, supporting their kids, while I was stood idle.

"Luckily, Winston was there, waving at me. I felt a slight relief, but it did not replace the sadness I felt. The announcer stood up at the podium, and began to speak. 'After careful consideration of all designs, we have done a thorough review of everything and have decided to go with Miss Whitmore's designs.' The crowd started to cheer, while Miss Whitmore's parents gave her a congratulatory hug. I was in disbelief; Miss Whitmore was my rival during my early teenage years, and, later as an adult. I was shocked, while she glanced my way, waving her trophy and prizes at me, to ensure that I was watching.

"As the competition ended and everyone left, she approached me. 'I know you expected to win. Regardless, where are your parents? They never come to support your events.' She said to me.

"I became angry because she knew how much the absence of my parents affected me. While I stood there on the verge of exploding, Winston drew me by the hand and said, 'It is time to head home.' From that point, the competition between Miss Whitmore and me grew even stronger. She was my next-door neighbor when my fashion career took flight; and she also helped me when I was obtaining a teaching certificate, which is the paradox of it all. She was my teacher, and helped me graduate from the program.

"So, the moral is to never let your background interfere with your destiny. My parents left me to my own devices many times. I understand your frustrations AJ, the key is to never lose hope.

"Well, what happened to Miss Whitmore?" AJ asked, as the story fed his curiosity.

"In the end, Miss Whitmore became my teacher and mentor." Miss Berta replied. The sky darkened outside the kitchen window. Miss Berta stood up from her seat. "I should be going. Please think about what I've said." She said to AJ.

12

THE GIFTED PROGRAM

Principal Hawk received Miss Berta's application for a full-time position. Miss Berta's credentials were outstanding. Miss Berta and Principal Hawk came to an agreement, that during Miss Berta's time as a substitute teacher, she would initiate a gifted program. Miss Berta had received a teaching certificate with an outstanding reference letter from Mrs. Whitmore. She also owned a top-selling magazine, which would be beneficial for the school's reputation. Miss Berta promoted West Brook High in a positive light.

Principal Hawk believed Miss Berta was the ideal candidate for the substitute teacher position. She took the high road and hired Miss Berta, after going back and forth on the decision several times. She feared that her position as principal would be questioned if she did not consider Miss Berta as the new substitute teacher. She knew that not accepting her would be headline news in the daily newspaper, because Miss Berta was affiliated with *Miss Berta and the Family Magazine,* which was extremely popular in the community. She was widely known throughout New York City. Miss Berta received the telephone call from Principal Hawk.

"Thank you, Principal Hawk. I'll see you bright and early tomorrow morning."

Miss Berta replied, cautiously hanging up the phone, while she began screaming with excitement.

Miss Berta arrived at West Brook High school, the same school AJ attends. Being part of the teaching faculty at West Brook High School, Miss Berta created a small group of students who had separate, private teaching lessons. She wanted to initiate this program and make it exclusive for the three percent of students, who were making satisfactory grades or above satisfactory level. Any student who achieved below satisfactory level, were placed into another classroom.

AJ was an exception for West Brook High School, in terms of test scores. The standardized test scores from this school were the lowest in the city. AJ was the brightest in his class, he started to read at a very early stage in life, before the other first graders, and this launched him ahead of his fellow classmates.

Miss Berta had a long conversation with Principal Hawk that morning, discussing her wishes regarding this gifted program. She wanted to initiate this program into the school's curriculum. She placed the few students who achieved the minimum or above the grade point average into the program.

The conversation did not sit too well with Principal Hawk, who was an army veteran who served in the military for four years. She was a strict disciplinarian, especially in regard to routine and structure. Change was something she did not like.

"Absolutely not!" Principal Hawk was outraged at the suggestion of a gifted program. Miss Berta did not know where to take the conversation. She and Principal Hawk had a foul argument, exploiting other children who would not be in the same program, nor get the same level of education.

Later in the day, Miss Berta arrived home. She threw down her briefcase in frustration. Her cell phone was ringing off the hook. She immediately put her phone on mute and went into the kitchen. She placed her hands over her face and sighed. She walked over to the fridge, opened the long handle, and took out a pack of raw chicken fillets. Cooking was one of Miss Berta's hobbies. It was a way for her to continually be creative without being judged. Opening the kitchen cabinet, Miss Berta got seasonings from the cabinet and began sprinkling the poultry with paprika, seasoned salt, and black pepper. She added some squash and mashed potatoes to a broiling pan to accompany the meal. When the meal was ready, she got out her best china plate, which was beautifully designed with blue flowers.

She sat down at her beautiful table, and took a moment to meditate. She began to bless the food before she consumed it. She bowed her head in prayer, and took her time, while she slowly enjoyed every bite. While chewing on some squash, she dropped her fork on her plate, and rushed over to the telephone to dial Leticia's number. Leticia answered immediately.

"Miss Berta what's been going on? I haven't seen nor heard from you in a few days. Why haven't you been to work? I was worried, I even considered stopping by your home to check up on you and see if you were all right!" Leticia announced, in a hushed tone.

Miss Berta interrupted Leticia, who was going a mile a minute with her words of concern.

"I am working on the Johnson case," Miss Berta announced to Leticia confidently.

"What? Why?" Leticia responded inquisitively. Miss Berta explained there would be days, when she wouldn't be showing up to the headquarters of *Miss Berta and the Family Magazine*. After her long discussion with Leticia, Miss Berta hung up the phone.

Many days passed since Leticia and Miss Berta spoke on topics concerning the magazine. On a Saturday morning, Miss Berta sat down in her living room with her laptop on her lap and began typing an email to Mr. Bill, the investor of *Miss Berta and the Family*. It read:

> *Dear Mr. Bill,*
> *I humbly regret to inform you, that I plan to take a month off from the magazine, to serve as a substitute teacher for West Brook High School. This opportunity, which I recently received, will give me the interviews and knowledge, in regard to what should be featured in the magazine. Please understand that this opportunity at West Brook High School will take the magazine to a new plateau. I will definitely keep you posted on our efforts.*
> *Sincerely,*
> *Miss Berta London*
> *Chief Editor, Miss Berta and the Family Magazine.*

13

THE NEW JOB

The following day, Miss Berta got up early to collect the mail. Flex Delivery was a delivery package company. Their truck had been parked outside Miss Berta's house. Miss Berta walked outside, while the Flex Delivery man waved at her while he delivered a package to Miss Berta's neighbors. She ignored the deliveryman. He made her nervous, she dropped the pile of mail she was carrying. Embarrassed, she quickly picked up the mail and hurried into the house, slamming the door behind her.

Miss Berta's first day of teaching arrived. She was in her simple brown blazer, black pumps, briefcase, handbag, and was on her way to her teaching job at West Brook High School. Principal Hawk and Miss Berta decided to put their differences aside, and work together as a team. Miss Berta was granted permission to do as she pleased academically in the classroom, as long as the student's grades improved.

Upon arrival, Miss Berta discovered the high school AJ attended was a completely different world. The students stared at her, as she rolled into the parking lot in her flashy car. It wasn't until Miss Berta stepped out of the car, that a group of young students whistled at her in a derogatory way, she was frightened. The high school boys were muscular in size. They looked like weight lifters. As the new authority figure in town, Miss Berta showed no sign of fear.

"One more word and detention with the principal!" Miss Berta retorted at the young high school boys. The young boys laughed among themselves, it wasn't until Principal Hawk came out, that each one regained their proper decorum. "I see when you arrive that things are under control." Miss Berta said.

Miss Berta smiled at Principal Hawk. She loved her authoritative position.

As the students hurried inside the building, Principal Hawk took Miss Berta to the side and began discussing the rules and regulations of the school. They approached the 12D classroom. Principal Hawk walked inside, followed by Miss Berta. AJ was seated in the front center of the classroom. His backpack was on the floor beside him. He was in the process of drawing an animated character on his notebook with his pencil. The other students were boisterous and very dramatic. Some threw paper planes, while the other students danced on the tables.

"Mr. Thompson! Get off that table immediately!" Principal Hawk scolded. A small boy quickly jumped off the table and sat in his seat. "Settle down, class!" Principal Hawk insisted.

The students stopped what they were doing and got into their seats, except for two girls, who were arguing about who got the middle seat.

"Janice and Anna, ladies, sit down anywhere!" Principal Hawk instructed. Janice took the first seat and Anna smugly took the other. Principal Hawk introduced Miss Berta, while she started explaining where she was from, and the reasons she decided to become a teacher. It wasn't long afterward Principal Hawk finished her introduction. She was on her way out of the classroom, when students resumed their discussions and danced on their desks. Principal Hawk quickly turned her head around, to look inside the classroom, "That is quite enough!" She scolded.

Miss Berta was astonished at the students' atrocious behavior. She walked to AJ's desk, to give him a planner. The planner was divided by months, weeks and the entire school year. AJ became embarrassed. He placed his head on his desk in hiding, as the other students made fun of him.

"The new boy has a crush on the substitute teacher!" A boy in the back row mocked, as the other students laughed aloud. Miss Berta tried to get the class under control. She began to raise her voice.

"Would everyone keep quiet?" Miss Berta screamed.

"You keep quiet! Matter of fact, shut up!" A boy on the table yelled back, while the other students laughed. Miss Berta didn't know what to do. She was impulsive; she rushed to the fire alarm and pulled it down. The students ran crazily out of the classroom. They were headed toward the exit of the school. They were excited, yet anxious as fire trucks pulled up in front of the school. Principal Hawk got everyone assembled. Miss Berta was one of the last people to exit the building. The firemen cautiously guided the students and teachers off the premises. It wasn't long afterward, parents showed up to pick up their children. An hour later, the firemen came and told Principal Hawk that it was a false alarm. Principal Hawk sent the students home early because of the news.

The next day, Principal Hawk was on a quest to find out who falsely rang the fire alarm. Miss Berta wandered into Principal Hawk's office to tell her that she did it, to get the students to settle down. With the exception of AJ, none of them would listen to her. She explained that she pulled the fire alarm, because the students were standing on tables.

Principal Hawk sat patiently listening. Once Miss Berta finished her drawn out explanation, Principal Hawk was not pleased. She got straight to the point and came down on Miss Berta like a ton of bricks. "Miss Berta, if you don't keep a handle on your students, you won't last long here. You are officially a substitute teacher. *Contain your classroom!*" Principle Hawk denounced. Miss Berta knew she had to straighten up her teaching methods, and get her classroom under control at the quickest rate possible.

14

MISS BERTA MOVES INTO HER OLD HOUSE

On a Saturday morning, Miss Berta walked to her mailbox, which was located right outside of her home. She took an envelope from the mailbox and opened it, to find a check displaying *Miss Berta and the Family Magazine*, which was. in the amount of $1 million, with a Post-it on it reading: "Happy Payday!"—Mr. Bill, your investor.

This large paycheck was the incentive for Miss Berta to move back to her old home in Manhattan, which she missed dearly. She was able to buy the home back from Ned Robinson, as well her dogs. She did not have Alexis, Christine, and Cephas, her old staff. The move into her old home required assistance from her old friends, the Williamson children.

Miss Berta dialed the Williamson's home number, Jessica picked up the phone call and immediately recognized Miss Berta's voice.

"Miss Berta, what on earth? How are you? Where have you been?" Jessica questioned, without taking a breath.

"Well, if you calm down, I may be able to explain everything to you," Miss Berta replied, while Jessica was silent, intent on listening. "I am moving, back into my old house. Do you and Nick wish to help me?"

"Absolutely," Jessica replied excitedly, on the other line.

"All right, inform your mother and let me know. I move in tomorrow, so let me know sometime tomorrow," Miss Berta replied, as she hung up the phone.

The next morning, Miss Berta heard the doorbell ring. She quickly rushed down the large stairway, and opened the front door. The Williamson family stood at her doorstep. Miss Berta's eyes immediately lit up. "What on earth are you all doing here?" She asked.

Mrs. Williamson smiled. " Jessica said you were moving into your old home, and we want to repay you for bringing our family together. We wish to assist you with your move. Allow us to do so." Mrs. Williamson insisted.

Mr. Williamson placed Johnny on the floor, while he shook Miss Berta's hand. "Mr. Williamson, it is definitely a surprise to see you. Thank you so much for your assistance." Miss Berta smiled, as she directed the family into her bare living room. Johnny was running around the room, while Nick chased after him.

"Where do we begin?" Jessica asked pensively.

"Well, I am currently waiting for the deliverers. They should be here any moment." Miss Berta replied.

Suddenly, the doorbell rang again, five men stood before Miss Berta, as she answered the door. "Ah, right on time, gentlemen." One of the men gave Miss Berta a clipboard for her to sign her name. She took the clipboard and signed her name, and gave it back. All of the five men hurried back to the truck, which was parked outside the driveway. They began bringing boxes into the living room.

Mrs. Williamson began to give out orders. "Those boxes go into the kitchen," she instructed, while she grabbed the clipboard from one of the deliverymen. She read aloud what it had said. "Color-coordinated for each department: kitchen, living room, bedroom, office, and bathroom.

"That goes in the kitchen sir," Mrs. Williamson instructed two men, who had boxes in their arms. They began to make their way toward the kitchen. Meanwhile, Mr. Williamson was opening boxes and helping the men bring furniture into the house. He also assisted with rearranging the furniture.

Meanwhile, the doorbell rang. Miss Berta walked to the door, opened it, and found AJ at the doorstep. "AJ, how are you?" Miss Berta asked. She welcomed him inside her home. "I am thrilled to see you, but what brings you here?" She asked.

"Leticia, your assistant said you needed help with the move." AJ replied. He spotted Jessica and waved at her. She waved back at him. Miss Berta noticed her parents glance their way.

"This is one of my students, he goes to the school where I currently substitute teach," Miss Berta said by way of introduction.

"Pleasure to meet you, young man," Mr. Williamson replied, as he approached AJ. He resumed to his duty, repositioning the furniture in the living room. Mrs. Williamson took no notice of AJ. She continued to direct the deliverymen, so they could distribute the remaining items. Miss Berta walked up to Mrs. Williamson, to introduced them to one another. "This is AJ," Miss Berta said to Mrs. Williamson, who turned to face them.

"Hello AJ. I'm a bit busy at the moment. Jessica can be more acquainted with you. You both are around the same age," Mrs. Williamson replied. Jessica approached AJ, while Miss Berta went to check on Nick and Johnny, who were helping their father open boxes and unpack items.

Jessica shook AJ's hand, while he stood idle. "Hello, how are you?" Jessica questioned.

"Good." AJ responded.

"So, what brings you here?" Jessica anticipated.

Well, I'm here to help Miss Berta with her move."

"Awesome, well you can give me a hand, while we unpack some of these boxes," Jessica instructed.

"So, I finally meet you in person." AJ said.

"So, what college are you going to? What are your goals in life?" Jessica inquired.

"Well, I wish to do an internship before I go to college." AJ said, while Jessica's eyes widened.

"Really? So am I. I'm actually going to Geneva, Switzerland," Jessica boasted.

AJ's face saddened. "You're lucky, I wish I could go to Switzerland." AJ replied.

"What do you mean?" Jessica responded.

"I don't have the money to go," AJ admitted.

Miss Berta couldn't help, but overhear the conversation. "AJ, not to worry. I'll take care of it," Miss Berta interrupted. AJ looked at Miss Berta, bewildered.

"I cannot accept that offer," AJ responded.

"Well, I just heard the two of you speaking and it would be a terrific idea for you to go to Geneva, Switzerland for an internship. I will help you with the application and expense." Miss Berta replied.

"We think it's a good idea," Mrs. Williamson admitted.

"We will also chip in. I always like to help, especially when I have the means to do so," Mr. Williamson interrupted.

"Well AJ, you have the support to apply to the internship. All of us will chip in, to help you get there," Miss Berta announced. Nick and Johnny clapped their hands together. They were just as excited as everyone else.

15

FLEX DELIVERY MAN

Miss Berta's first few days at West Brook High School were disastrous. She had made a bad impression on Principal Hawk, who was waiting for the right moment to dismiss her.

After a long day, Miss Berta headed straight home from work. She got out of the car, unloaded her briefcase, and hurried to her front door. A Flex Delivery truck was parked outside her house. A handsome, dark-haired man stood outside her doorway. Miss Berta found him attractive, but she did not take his looks too seriously.

"What are you doing outside my door?" Miss Berta snapped.

"I have a package for you miss," the Flex Delivery man stumbled. He was quite nervous talking to Miss Berta because of her piercing eyes and style of dress, which was so distinctive. He couldn't understand why he was attracted to such a strange woman, but he was, and it showed all over his face. Miss Berta was equally interested, but did a great job hiding her emotions. She could not be distracted, she was a substitute teacher and her time was preoccupied.

The following day, Miss Berta brought books from famous philosophers: Plato, Aristotle, Socrates, and many others to West Brook High School. As she passed the copies around, she told her class to pick a portion of the books to photocopy. The students rebelled. They didn't want to do the homework assignments. AJ was the only one skimming through a book, a portion of Plato. The other students threw their books down on their desks.

Miss Berta decided it was the last straw. *"Everyone who does not wish to do the assignment, get out!"*

The students were in shock. They did not budge from their seats. Most of them knew they could not go home, fearing the reactions from their parents.

The leader of the obnoxious students was Roland Tim, a slim boy well known for his basketball skills. He picked up his book and did as Miss Berta instructed. Many students around school knew if anyone were to be recruited into the NBA, it would be Roland Tim. The only problem with Roland was that his grades were insufficient. The students followed him, and picked out their excerpts from the philosophy books for their next class discussion.

Miss Berta decided to do research on each student. Her goal was to research their family history. She stayed late at West Brook High School daily, assessing all the student files. Cameron Henderson was musically inclined—she sang. Ruth Burns was interested in dressing up in the latest fashion trends. Robert Nixon was interested in business; he constantly sold candy and snacks at lunch. He came to school with a camping backpack on his back, filled with goods. The students always came to him to buy candy, chips, or whatever he had on that specific day.

Miss Berta felt it was her duty to guide the students, to pursue their passions in a respectful way. It was a tough task to motivate these children. There were days when the students got fed up with their classes, and preferred to sleep during class or throw books on the floor. Miss Berta's main plan was to observe the students after school, to get a better understanding of how to help them.

AJ was her first pursuit, he had been the main reason she wanted to teach at West Brook High School. She constantly asked him to stay several days after school, so she could coach him for the aptitude tests, which were just around the corner. The other students made fun of him during this process. One of the students walked past the classroom and yelled, "Dude, check out Miss Berta and AJ!" The teasing was overwhelming for AJ to handle. He had no one he could confide in, and felt ostracized because he had no friends.

Two weeks before AJ was scheduled for his aptitude exam, he quit the aptitude coaching because of the constant teasing he received from his peers.

Miss Berta came home aggravated, to find the Flex Delivery Man, Travis Jenson, who knocked on the door with a package. "Rough day?" He inquired calmly.

"Why do you ask sir?" Miss Berta replied impatiently.

"It shows," he responded as he crossed his arms.

Miss Berta didn't know how to take his reaction, "How dare you!" Miss Berta snapped harshly at Travis.

"I've been meaning to ask you, what are in these packages?" Travis asked boldly.

"I order books online for my students." Miss Berta replied. She gradually became comfortable around Travis. She vented about the unruly students she had to teach continually. Travis and Miss Berta talked about the pressures of running a magazine, and teaching high school students. Travis waited at the doorstep for Miss Berta each day, to give her words of encouragement.

"You seem like the type of woman who can handle anything." Travis smiled. These words of encouragement uplifted Miss Berta. He made jokes about certain incidents that happened at West Brook High School, which Miss Berta laughed at hysterically.

Travis had once been engaged to the love of his life, a Frenchwoman named Madeline, who ran off with another man. This left Travis scared to get into a deep and personal relationship. However, he felt comfortable with Miss Berta. She added happiness to his life. One late afternoon, she arrived home to find Travis waiting on the doorstep, with a bouquet of sunflowers. Miss Berta smiled. "What is all this about?" She asked shyly, he simply smiled back at her.

"I just want you to know that my feelings for you are growing," Travis confessed. The love connection between Travis and Miss Berta grew stronger from that point.

16

ON TOP OF THINGS

Miss Berta began putting her thoughts in motion, concerning how she was going to help every student in her classroom. She took the class on field trips, which she paid for out of her own pocket. Some of the students never had the opportunity travel to the countryside, or beyond their community. Some students stood outside the school building, not too far away from West Brook High School. They hung around the block all day, never attending class, and knew nothing beyond their hometown. Miss Berta wanted to change that, she wanted to get to know these students; so she could be a positive influence in their lives. They were her students; it was her duty to guide them.

AJ was on his way to school, a mob of five teenage boys approached him, demanding his backpack. His immediate response was, *"No! Get your own!"*

The mob was shocked by his response. They broke his nose and left him with two black eyes. AJ was unable to go on the trip, Miss Berta was alarmed because AJ did not show up for the field trip, nor did he show up for school the following day. Three days later, she noticed AJ was not at school. She grew concerned.

That afternoon, Miss Berta went to AJ's home, and knocked on the door. AJ's mother screamed at her. Before Miss Berta could get a word in, AJ walked across the room in pain.

"Leave it alone, Mom!" AJ shouted angrily. At that point, the door was slammed in Miss Berta's face, before she got the chance to speak. Miss Berta courageously knocked on the door once more, Henrietta quickly swung the door open, and the yelling started once again.

Miss Berta stood still, but inside she was exploding with anger. "Be quiet, please!" Miss Berta pushed past Henrietta, while AJ was on the couch, wrapped in a blanket, watching TV. Henrietta was stunned, because she did not say another word. She was aware that Miss Berta was looking out for AJ's best interests. Otherwise, she would not have shown up at his house. Miss Berta gave AJ's paperwork concerning the application for the internship in Geneva, Switzerland. AJ took the paperwork and smiled. "Fill this out and give it back to me?" Miss Berta asked AJ.

She left the house, and AJ did not hesitate to fill out the paperwork. At the top of the application, he filled out his name and date of birth and below began to answer the essay question: Please describe your goals for the future. What is your five-year plan? Provide information concerning your grades, and where you wish to attend college. AJ's admission essay read:

> *My name is AJ Johnson,*
> *I live in Brooklyn, New York. I am not from the best neighborhood, but I am a survivor. The world of academia has saved my life. It has exposed me to ideas and concepts that are not encountered on my side of town. There is a low graduation rate in my high school, but I want to be part of the statistic that escapes. I want to go to college. I believe this internship will pave my way to become a doctor in social work. I wish to help my community and my fellow students get up out of this usual routine. Again my name is AJ Johnson. I am the top of my class, with the highest grade point average. Miss Berta London, the former editor for Eloquent Fashion Magazine is my teacher. She has inspired me to be all that I am, which is a survivor. I am a very hard worker. I have worked my entire life precisely. My goal is to attend Vine University in Boston and study architecture and design.*
> *Sincerely, AJ Johnson.*

The following week, Miss Berta stopped by AJ's home, to give him some SAT exercises for the upcoming week. He gave Miss Berta the internship application, which she mailed to Geneva on the day she received it.

AJ was due back in school on Monday, but he couldn't go anywhere because of his serious injuries. As the week progressed, AJ slowly recovered. Miss Berta brought AJ his homework and aptitude prep exercises each day to his home.

Henrietta began to appreciate Miss Berta's code of ethics. She discovered that Miss Berta had been a well-known fashion icon, before she created the family magazine, and this impressed her. She looked to her as a source of inspiration for her son, and for herself. She perceived Miss Berta as a strong woman, who had overcome so much in her lifetime.

AJ returned to his usual self the following Monday, things began to change for him. The students at school looked to him as a leader, and saw that he was destined for greatness. The students wanted to be more like AJ. They wanted to study harder and get better grades. The boys asked him to tutor them, and so did the girls. They wanted to believe that their dreams would also be attainable. AJ came from poverty, yet worked while in school. He was receiving all of his homework at home during his injury, and still was top of his class. The students respected him for this. They gossiped about him all the time, and overheard Principal Hawk talk to the other teachers about it.

Recruiters made a visit to the West Brook High School. Roland Tim, the captain of the basketball team, was in for a rude awakening. He was warned that the recruitment date was approaching. If his grades did not improve, he would have no chance of getting recruited into a college basketball team.

It was a Tuesday morning; AJ sat at his desk in the front row of the classroom. Roland Tim sat behind him and whispered into his ear, "So, do you get straight As in math?" He asked.

"Yes I do," AJ responded.

"Can you tutor me sometime?" Roland asked impatiently.

AJ nodded his head in surprise and smiled. He hoped a friendship would prosper out of this arrangement. Roland Tim was considered the most popular boy in school. Although he didn't want to get his hopes too high, he couldn't help himself.

After class, Roland Tim hung out by the lockers laughing, making jokes with his basketball buddies. AJ was nervous, but deep inside he was a big fan of Roland Tim. He wished he had learned to play basketball as well as the other boys his age could. He had a deep love for the game. AJ gathered his courage and walked right up to the West Brook High School basketball team.

Roland Tim looked at him with curiosity. The players crossed their arms, staring at AJ.

"Hey, Roland Tim, can I talk to you for a second?" AJ mumbled to Roland.

A boy called Harrison, who was part of the team, responded nastily, "Yo, Roland Tim, this loser wants to have a word with you."

The team laughed at the remark. Roland Tim pushed Harrison out of the way.

"Dude! What's your problem?" Harrison replied, shocked by the fact that he'd been pushed by one of his teammates. The players gasped in surprise and decided to leave. As they walked away, Roland Tim smiled. "What is it, AJ?" He asked.

"I was wondering if I you can teach me to play basketball? I want to try out for the team. " AJ replied.

Roland Tim looked at AJ in shock. He couldn't believe what he was being asked. The smartest boy in school with the highest grades actually cared to play sports. It was the strangest thing he had ever heard. It took a moment for Roland Tim to understand, but he eventually did and nodded his head sporadically, accepting the request.

AJ was excited that his life in high school was going to change for the better. Roland Tim stayed after school and AJ tutored him, giving him math problems to complete for their next meeting. On Saturdays, AJ met with Roland Tim on the basketball court. The team practiced for hours on end. It didn't bother AJ. He picked up new tricks and techniques, and enjoyed watching the entire team play.

The practices were intense, there was lots of yelling and usually a team member would leave because he could not accept a foul. At times, these scenarios were entertaining, but not when the game ended and a team member walked off the court.

Some days, the team packed up and went home early, this enabled AJ to have some one-on-one practice time with Roland Tim. AJ learned how to intercept the ball. He also learned how to defend his side of the court. Roland Tim went above and beyond during practice lessons, while he trained AJ because he was eager to learn.

One day after one of their basketball practice session, Roland Tim decided to take AJ to a local shoe store called Nicks, a lower-priced store, where a lot of the neighborhood kids went to buy sneakers. Roland Tim showed AJ a few pairs of sneakers. "What is so special about them? Is it the low prices?" AJ inquired.

"That is what most people think about these shoes, but the secret is that they make you feel light as a feather. Please get yourself a pair," Roland Tim persuaded him. AJ did not hesitate. He bought them with the money he had saved from working in the restaurant. The money was meant to help his mother pay the rent this month, but he would just tell her he didn't have money to do so, and hopefully she would understand. It made her upset, because she would have to work overtime, but in order to achieve success, he had to buy these sneakers.

Roland Tim's math skills excelled with each tutoring session, both benefited. AJ's basketball skills improved, he became such a good player. Roland Tim asked AJ to become part of the basketball team at West Brook High School. He decided to ask the head coach to make it possible. The head coach agreed and AJ was happy to be part of the team and have friends. The basketball team grew enthusiastic, and became friends with him. AJ's confidence grew, he felt good about his chances to excel on the aptitude test, and get into a good college. He was also going to get the Sconzy, the notebook laptop Miss Berta promised him.

17

MISS BERTA DOESN'T MIND HER BUSINESS

Principal Hawk walked past classroom 12D and noticed how involved the students had become. Miss Berta gave them projects to spark their interests. They were enthralled with their poetry assignments; she had them attempt to draw heartfelt images expressing the messages the poets were trying to convey. Miss Berta walked around the class, observing the students. She approached a young timid boy with brown hair.

"What does this poem mean to you?" Miss Berta asked.

"Well as I was reading the poem, I decided to draw trees surrounded by pigs and wolves, because I feel each animal is attacking it and the tree is helpless," the student explained, as he placed down the picture of his drawing beside the poem.

"Nicely done, keep up the great work." Miss Berta replied. Meanwhile, Principal Hawk walked inside the classroom. Each student paused their assignments and acknowledged Principal Hawk. Miss Berta greeted the principal.

"Hello, Principal Hawk, how are you doing today?" She asked. Principal Hawk simply ignored her and walked around the classroom to observe the work from each student, while Miss Berta interrupted her.

"We are currently reading poems and drawing images to convey the messages of the poems."

"I did not ask for an information session. When I do, by all means do explain, but for now I would like to maintain the silence," Principal Hawk explained to Miss Berta, who did not dare to interrupt her again.

"Listen Miss Berta. I respect your intentions, but you must understand we cannot afford the resources. The district has cut funding from our school, and we have to make cuts." Principal Hawk replied.

Miss Berta arrived home from work to find Henrietta standing outside with no shoes on. Her dress was drenched from the rain, and she wore a frightened expression. Miss Berta calmly and rationally maintained her composure, but she was deeply concerned.

"Is AJ all right?" Miss Berta gasped, Henrietta nodded her head slowly. She couldn't restrain herself, tears streamed down her face.

"I'm sorry to impose, I called your office and your assistant gave me your home address. I told her it was urgent." Henrietta sobbed, while Miss Berta quickly got out her house keys from her purse, and invited Henrietta into her home. She escorted her toward her big, eighteenth century–style chair located in the living room.

Miss Berta wasn't sure how to handle the situation, she simply asked, "What happened?" Henrietta dissolved into tears, stumbling over her words. She began to explain cautiously.

"AJ was bragging to me about his accomplishments on the aptitude tests. He was in the process of waiting for his scores. I told him I was proud, regardless of the outcome. It was at that point Lucas became aggressive. He threw things around. AJ jumped on Lucas's back to stop him, while Lucas threw him to the ground and told him that if he got involved, he would hurt him so bad that college would not even be an option for him. I told my son to go to a movie, while I took care of Lucas, but he was reluctant to leave. I pleaded with him for quite some time. The moment AJ walked out the door, Lucas became out of control. The lamp was thrown, he was punching the walls." Henrietta continued.

Miss Berta was in shock. She had her hands over her mouth. Henrietta continued to explain why Lucas was not making her happy, and that her happiness was an illusion. Although Miss Berta did not know Lucas, it was clear that he was not interested in anyone or anything, but himself and his own gain.

After hearing Henrietta's story, Miss Berta understood why the Johnsons were a dysfunctional family. Lucas was the weakest link in the family chain. He took all of the attention from AJ, so he could have Henrietta to himself. This explained why so much responsibility fell on AJ's shoulders. This annoyed Miss Berta, she wanted to do everything in her power to rid the family of Lucas. She straightened up her posture and asked Henrietta if she would like a cup of tea. Humbly, Henrietta nodded and replied, "Yes please, thank you." Miss Berta went into the kitchen, gathered some shortbread biscuits and cranberry-apricot tea. Henrietta began to feel slightly relieved at the sight of the tea and biscuits, but was still stressed. Miss Berta handed her one of the teacups and poured the tea, while Miss Berta began to counsel her.

"Henrietta, you have to leave Lucas, not only for your safety, but for AJ's well-being. He's your only son. Lucas is a weak link that will destroy your family." Miss Berta said.

Henrietta sobbed hysterically, she was afraid of Lucas. It was visible in her eyes, especially when she spoke of him. Miss Berta explained that fear prevented people from pursuing courageous lives. She was direct with Henrietta, who absorbed the encouraging words. Henrietta prepared herself to leave Miss Berta's home. She turned to face her.

"Miss Berta thank you. I needed you to get through this." She said to Miss Berta, who gave her a warm hug.

The following night, Miss Berta lay awake in her bed, thinking of the different possibilities to help AJ escape from his tormenting life. The first person that came to mind was her old employee Romero. She picked up the phone by her bedside table, and called him.

"Romero?" Inquired Miss Berta over the phone.

"Who is this?" The voice on the line replied.

"Miss Berta." She responded.

Romero could not believe this surprise.

"How is everything going at *Elle Magazine*?" Miss Berta asked in order to break the silence. Romero hesitated, as he gathered his thoughts.

"Different, very different."

"Different is good, different is always good," Miss Berta replied.

"What brings you to make this phone call Miss Berta?" Romero asked out of curiosity.

"I need you to do a favor for me, for old time's sake." Miss Berta asked desperately.

Romero paused for a brief moment. "Sure, I'll do it." He replied.

Romero was invited on her behalf, to help AJ with his self-esteem.

"Romero, I need you to educate AJ on style, he needs fashion, as a confidence booster; a whole new wardrobe is the ticket. Basketball has made him semi-confident, but fashion will complete the process." Miss Berta instructed.

Days later, Romero entered Miss Berta's home. Miss Berta introduced him to the Johnson family. "Hi, everyone, this is my most trusted former colleague Romero." He said.

"Hi Romero," Henrietta and AJ replied in unison.

"Kid, the fashion industry isn't about what you wear. It's about how you wear the clothing, and how you feel inside when you wear it," Romero said.

AJ listened intensively to Romero's advice, he was aware of Romero's status from working at *Elle Magazine*. Romero had stacks of men clothing, that he brought with him to give to AJ. He was in shock at the prospect of free clothes.

"I want you to wear this orange shirt with these white pants." Romero instructed.

"Are these from Moi Designs?" AJ asked.

"They certainly are," Romero announced.

AJ shook his head in disbelief. "Now, this is awesome." He replied. Miss Berta walked into the room with Henrietta following behind her. "Can we be of any assistance?" She asked.

Henrietta gasped when she witnessed AJ's transformation. "You look so handsome my son," Henrietta announced. Miss Berta smiled at Romero, while AJ bestowed a look of respect toward Miss Berta.

"I can't believe it's you," Miss Berta announced, facing AJ.

"Son?" Henrietta inquired. AJ faced his mother, surprised that the two were acquaintances.

"We've talked for a bit." Henrietta replied.

"Well, she does have a sense of fashion." AJ replied.

"Miss Berta is the epitome of the fashion world," Henrietta announced enthusiastically.

"What do you mean?" AJ responded.

Romero looked at AJ with disbelief. "She was the co-owner and editor-in-chief of *Eloquent Fashion Magazine*." Romero answered.

AJ was wide-eyed with shock. "No, are you serious?"

"Sure I am," Romero announced confidently.

"Why the change of careers?" AJ asked.

"Fashion is an industry that can consume you entirely. I wanted a change, to be part of something bigger than myself," she replied honestly.

AJ wanted to know more about Romero's background. "When did she employ you?" He asked.

"My story is interesting, Miss Berta found me at a car wash. I would stand in front of Lule's and encourage people to wash their cars. Her chauffeur at the time, Henry Conrad, was driving her. I walked up to the car and Miss Berta exited in her bright red hat and flat brown shoes. She was one serious woman. I asked her if she wanted to get her car washed. She simply said, 'Well, this is a car wash, isn't it?' 'Yes miss,' I responded.

"I guess she noticed my fashion sense. Out of all the employees at Lule Car Wash, I was the only one taking photographs of the cars. She walked up to me and said, 'Can I see them?' I showed her the digital photos I took. She simply gave me her card with her contact number on it. I called the next day, and she asked if I was interested in the fashion business, I immediately jumped at the opportunity, knowing it would change my life for the better." Romero confessed.

AJ was amazed. "Wow, who would have guessed, that one woman had all this power?"

"Yes, she changed lives. I was definitely one of the lucky ones, who had a crappy job at the start with a cheating girlfriend Anna," Romero replied.

"Why would you have a girlfriend who cheated on you?" AJ asked.

He crossed his arms with anticipation, while Romero reflected on his past life. "Fear of loneliness." He inquired.

AJ put his head down. "Tell me about it."

Inquisitively, Romero stared at AJ. "Do you have girl troubles too?" He asked.

"I didn't have girl troubles until my ex-girlfriend started dating a boy on the basketball team," AJ replied.

"Do you want her back?" Romero asked AJ cautiously.

"I do miss her. Seeing her with that boy on the team does make me want to come to her rescue. Hot girls don't usually go for the nerds, anyway." AJ said.

"Let's change that!" Romero snapped. Shocked, AJ did not understand what Romero implied. "You will feel comfortable in your own skin, just follow the color scheme I have laid out for you," Romero announced.

"Blue collared shirts, jeans. White pants, I can wear with any shirt," AJ replied.

"Exactly! These bags of clothes should serve you well." Romero answered as he picked up his backpack, sunglasses, and his water, while he said a brief good-bye to the group.

"Thank you, Romero," Miss Berta said, as he was leaving.

"Pleasure, I am entirely indebted to you. You saved me from that car wash job, I would have had it for my entire life, had you not intervened." Romero smiled, while Miss Berta smiled back.

"You've done very well for yourself," Romero declared.

"So have you." AJ said.

The following day, AJ attended school with sailor boat shoes given to him by Romero, along with white pants and an orange shirt. He was the main topic for gossip. Elena was a short girl, who was very quiet with brown hair and happened to be Rebecca's best friend. Rebecca was tall with an outgoing personality. They ran down the hallway, which was packed with students, talking among themselves. Elena and Rebecca ran toward Ariana, who was AJ's ex-girlfriend.

"Did you see your ex-boyfriend today?" Elena asked excitedly.

"What on earth are you talking about, Elena?" Rebecca responded.

"AJ, he's different." Elena persisted.

Worried, Rebecca grabbed hold of Elena. "Oh my gosh, is he okay?" Elena began pulling away, and indicated for Rebecca to turn around. Standing behind Rebecca was AJ, looking debonair in his new attire.

"How are you, Rebecca?" AJ asked smugly.

Rebecca gasped in astonishment at AJ's transformation. Smiling at AJ, she responded shyly, "AJ, I had no idea you were standing behind me. Well, you look different." He said.

"Handsomely different?" AJ corrected her.

Rebecca laughed at AJ's bold joke. "You wish. Well you do look nice."

"Thank you Rebecca," AJ responded happily. "You know, it's been a long while since we broke up," he reminded her.

Rebecca became embarrassed, she turned her head away in shame. "How have you been?" She inquired.

"Studying hard, but not so good," he replied.

"What's wrong?" Rebecca asked.

"It's personal," AJ responded.

"How about we talk about it over lunch sometime?" Rebecca shyly asked.

"I don't think that's a good idea," AJ declared.

"Why not?" Rebecca responded.

"Your boyfriend won't approve," AJ remarked sarcastically. He walked away, while

Rebecca stood, puzzled.

Rebecca and Roland Tim started dating a few months ago. It was at the homecoming dance. Rebecca anticipated that AJ would ask her to go with him. On Monday, classes lasted the usual hour in length. During lunch, Rebecca was sitting, and eating potato chips with her friends Elena, Torry, and Jenny. The boys from the basketball team grabbed their three bags of chips from the girls, which annoyed them.

Harrison was too busy occupying his time flirting with Elena. He blew innocent kisses toward her direction, and she responded coyly. Rebecca began to push Roland Tim away from her, as he grabbed her in a bear hug and would not let her go. "What are you going to do?" He reprimanded.

"If you do not release me, I swear you will never see the light of day," Rebecca replied smugly, laughing to herself.

Roland Tim was dominant. "I own you, Rebecca!"

Rebecca pushed away from Roland Tim's grip. "Nobody owns me. I own myself." She replied.

"Let's go for a walk downtown," Roland Tim interrupted.

"Fine." Rebecca pouted with her arms crossed in distaste.

The arguments between Roland Tim and Rebecca persisted over the next several weeks. Roland Tim felt superior at every moment. He put Rebecca in her sad mood swings.

Roland Tim held Rebecca's hand, squeezing it tightly. "Ouch, you're hurting me," Rebecca scolded Roland Tim, while she pushed him away.

Fury took over Roland Tim. He slapped Rebecca across the face and walked away from her. Rebecca froze, with her hands over her sensitive cheek. The following day in English class, AJ sat behind Rebecca, who was cradling her cheek once again. "Hey Rebecca, are you all right?" AJ asked, concerned.

"I'm *fine!*" Rebecca said, while she faced AJ. He blatantly looked at her with disappointment.

"I guess you and Roland Tim are not doing well?" He inquired.

Rebecca became annoyed at AJ's statement, and rushed from the classroom while the English teacher continued the lecture on Western Civilization. Feeling ashamed and embarrassed, AJ was repulsed by his statement toward Rebecca. He decided to follow her, while she sat in the hallway of the school's entrance, kneeling with her face covered.

"Rebecca, what is wrong? This is not like you," He stated.

Tears streamed down Rebecca's face. She missed AJ's presence.

AJ was bold. He gave Rebecca a big hug before she could resist his action of affection. "I'm here for you, tell me what is going on," AJ asked.

"He pushes me around, AJ!" She replied.

AJ was stunned. "What, where is he?" Rebecca began to restrain AJ, as the tears fell down her face.

"Come." AJ held out his hand to Rebecca.

"Where are we going?" Rebecca inquired.

"Meet me at the café after school?" He replied.

Rebecca smiled, and took AJ's hand. They both exited the school grounds hand in hand. They went to a small, brick, cottage-style café in a nicer part of town. The relaxing classical music of Antoine Dufoir played in the background, calmed Rebecca's spirits. AJ sat across from her, placing his hand over hers.

"Tell me everything," AJ said.

"AJ, there's nothing to tell," Rebecca responded.

"Please Rebecca, I'm worried about you," AJ said with concern.

"All right, well Roland Tim has been ruthlessly obnoxious these past couple of days," Rebecca answered.

"Rebecca, break up with him," AJ demanded.

"I definitely will consider it." She announced.

"No, just do it Rebecca. I don't want to see you suffer." AJ persisted.

Rebecca nodded her head in agreement

The following day, Miss Berta decided to take Henrietta out for a shopping excursion. Driving in Miss Berta's car, Henrietta had a lot of questions.

"How did you get into fashion?" Henrietta inquired.

"What do you know?" Miss Berta replied.

"AJ informed me about your former career in fashion." Henrietta replied.

Henrietta refrained from asking another question.

At King's Plaza, a shopping area in Brooklyn, Henrietta and Miss Berta looked at boutiques that sold handmade clothing.

"When did you get into the fashion industry?" Henrietta inquired.

Gasping, Miss Berta answered, "I was about three years old. Why do you ask?"

"Your fashion sense is impeccable," Henrietta confessed.

"Thank you Henrietta, lets take our mind off the topic for a while." Miss Berta replied graciously.

"What do you think of this green robe dress?" Henrietta modeled a long dress at the boutique.

"Hideous," Miss Berta reprimanded her.

"Shouldn't you be dressing your age?" Henrietta reminded her.

"Oh, keep quiet," Miss Berta shot back at her. Both of them began laughing.

18

THE TRANSITION PERIOD

Life began to change for AJ and Henrietta. Lucas was the only bad aspect of their life. He was an infectious plague, responsible for ruining the relationship between mother and son. Lucas took away the time Henrietta would spend with AJ, he was a demanding and selfish man who ignored AJ. Lucas was constantly in the background, nagging Henrietta about AJ. If AJ forgot to do something, or if his mother got into an argument with him, it usually ended with Lucas physically abusing Henrietta. There were days Henrietta couldn't walk because Lucas had beaten her so badly. He even instigated every situation, constantly arguing with Henrietta about AJ.

Tired of the sleepless nights, Henrietta decided to confront Lucas. She told AJ not to come home after school, warning him that she was going to confront Lucas, and she didn't want him to get in between their relationship. AJ became uncomfortable with this. It was not going to be easy, it was obvious that Lucas was not going to leave willingly.

That afternoon, Henrietta arrived home from work. Lucas was on the couch, waiting for dinner to be served. He was occupying himself watching ESPN football.

"I want tuna casserole today!" Lucas ordered, when Henrietta arrived at the house.

She walked into the kitchen, threw down her purse, and walked into the living room. "I'm sorry, Lucas, but this isn't going to work. I've tolerated you long enough," she spat. Lucas stared at Henrietta with his arms crossed. "You have to leave!" Henrietta announced.

"I'm not going anywhere. I help pay half the bills in this house!" Lucas responded.

"Paying a bill once does not count for paying the bills every month!"

Lucas got up from the couch and approached Henrietta with a severe, vicious look on his face. He slapped Henrietta, but she showed no sign of fear. "Well, I'm not going to leave!" Lucas blurted out.

"I'll have no choice but to involve the authorities if you do not decide to leave my home." Henrietta said.

At that point, Lucas knew Henrietta meant business. Without another word, Lucas walked into the back room to collect his belongings. He tucked some clothes in one arm and a small bag in the other, and left.

Lucas had not changed, in fact he was in and out of jobs, getting fired because he was late so many times, or he didn't show up at all. He insulted one of his supervisors. Henrietta influenced Lucas, but it didn't work. His stubborn personality always got the best of him, and he was resistant each time she made the effort to give him a written schedule, with a daily planner, to prepare his day.

Lucas was jealous of Henrietta. Though she was not a rich woman, he felt threatened, that she was an independent woman. It rubbed him the wrong way, because he could not take care of himself. He was jealous of AJ, whose intelligence exceeded his by miles. He knew AJ would get into a good college. He was getting many phone calls at home from various colleges nationwide. Lucas never mentioned these calls to AJ or Henrietta, it was eating Lucas up inside.

Henrietta's demands left him in a rage. He dropped his belongings outside on the front step, and went back inside the house and started destroying the home. Jealousy ate him up inside. He picked up furniture and started throwing it against the walls. He went into the kitchen, picked up plates by the masses, and shattered them on the floor. AJ appeared on the doorstep. Rushing inside, he heard his mother screaming. He did not say another word, as he dropped his backpack and went into his bedroom to pick up his baseball bat. Henrietta kept screaming, "AJ, don't do it!" He said.

AJ walked into the kitchen, holding his bat firmly in his hands. Lucas continued to destroy everything in his path. Meanwhile, AJ swung his bat and hit Lucas in the back. He collapsed with a loud yell, which scared AJ. He got back up, grabbed the bat from AJ, and started swinging it toward him. AJ fell to the ground. Before Lucas could swing a third time, Henrietta jumped on his back and bit him on the neck. Lucas tried to get her off his back, but he couldn't.

AJ was out cold, with a head bruise. Lucas had some cuts to his head. Meanwhile, Henrietta grabbed the bat from Lucas. She was furious at Lucas for threatening her son, and destroying their home. With the bat in her hand, Henrietta made an emergency call. A few minutes later, law enforcement officers were outside her house. Two tall men wore black jackets, along with black pants. Their badges were clearly visible. They both had stern looks on their faces. An ambulance carried AJ to the nearest hospital. Lucas was also carried away to the hospital.

Henrietta dialed Miss Berta's home number, and explained what happened to AJ and Lucas. She asked Miss Berta to come to Brooklyn, to help her answer some questions about the assaults that took place.

Miss Berta waited outside the police station, where Henrietta was being questioned. They asked if Lucas was her boyfriend. Her response was yes. Henrietta explained that Lucas to left her home because she wanted to move on with her life, and that he wasn't the right person for her. She went into detail about Lucas going berserk and destroying her home. A police officer opened the front door to the police station. He instructed Miss Berta to enter the building. The interview session with Henrietta had ended at that time. Miss Berta entered the interviewing room and was right beside Henrietta when she started crying. She gave her a hug, but Henrietta kept crying as she continued to explain the situation. The thought of AJ being injured was too much for her.

Finally, she calmed her nerves and began explaining how AJ witnessed the destructive path Lucas was on, and that AJ was just trying to defend her. The law enforcement officers listened while Henrietta finished explaining what happened.

19

MOTHER AND SON REUNITED

Miss Berta and Henrietta rushed to Lorrell Hospital, where AJ was being treated.

"Hi, we're here to see AJ Johnson." Henrietta was gasping for air as the words fell out of her mouth.

"The young boy who was brought here an hour ago?" An old, wrinkly receptionist inquired. Miss Berta and Henrietta nodded impatiently. "He's in E.R, on the first floor," the woman at the front desk replied.

Miss Berta and Henrietta ran down the hall. The hospital environment was quiet and peaceful. Henrietta and Miss Berta ran through the hospital, attracting attention from the patients. People grew deeply concerned about the two women sprinting through the halls. Suite A was closed. Henrietta did not knock on the door, but flung herself into Suite A. Miss Berta followed behind her. AJ lay there, bandaged from head to toe. Five hours had passed, and all Henrietta did was cry. Miss Berta placed her arms around Henrietta in an effort to comfort her, but it did not work. Henrietta was still upset. Miss Berta had her hands over her mouth, while tears streamed down her face. They couldn't believe AJ's condition. It took a few moments for him to speak. At that point, Henrietta and Miss Berta placed their arms over AJ in tears. "I'm okay," AJ mumbled to them, as he woke up.

Wiping her tears, Henrietta asked, "Are you really okay, son?"

"I'll be fine. I just need to see the doctor," AJ reassured her. Henrietta wiped her tears, while Miss Berta turned on the television. She noticed the images of the incident on the news. The images displayed Henrietta and Miss Berta rushing to the hospital. This made news because of the crowds of people, who stood outside Henrietta and AJ's home. Miss Berta gasped at the visuals. Henrietta shook her head in disgust. It wasn't until a few moments later, reporters appeared outside the Suite A door, taking pictures of AJ, Henrietta, and Miss Berta through the small window. Two security guards restrained the reporters from entering.

Miss Berta informed the hospital receptionist that it was an invasion of their privacy. Twenty minutes later, law enforcement officers entered the hospital. They restrained the crowd of reporters and blocked them from entering. Some of the reporters were aggressive and were escorted outside. The news caught on that Miss Berta was the high-profile editor from *Miss Berta and the Family Magazine.*

Later that evening, Miss Berta had asked Henrietta if she wanted her to stay at the hospital, but she did not wish to stay. She gave Henrietta and AJ a hug before she left. Henrietta stayed with AJ the whole night. She asked one of the nurses to get her an extra bed next to his. Henrietta and AJ had a long conversation concerning everything that happened in their lives. They discussed AJ's father leaving and why she had started dating Lucas. They cried and laughed together. It was truly a mother and son bonding moment.

Miss Berta was on her way home. Upon her arrival, she noticed a black SUV parked outside her house. It was Travis the Flex Delivery man. He was asleep in his car, waiting for Miss Berta's arrival. Miss Berta got out of the car and he woke up. "I saw you on TV. Is everything all right? I called your cell phone. I called your office, and grew deeply concerned," Travis announced. Miss Berta rushed into his arms and sobbed. Travis got out of the car and lifted her off the ground, picked up her briefcase, and carried her into the house. He placed her on the couch. She explained what took place at the Johnson home, while Travis took off her shoes and walked into the kitchen, getting ingredients out of the fridge to cook dinner.

Travis was the romantic type. He made sure Miss Berta was taken care of. Travis and Miss Berta had a lovely spaghetti dinner together, one that

Travis had prepared. The dining room was set with exquisite white candles, dimmed lighting, and some classical jazz music to set the mood. Miss Berta smiled at him. The entire evening cheered her up, but she was still very upset about AJ. Travis gave her reassurance, that things would be okay for him, because he was a strong boy to have survived.

Henrietta and AJ had dinner at the hospital that night. They had chicken filet with cheese and broccoli, rice with gravy, and a cherry dessert.

AJ's humor was back to normal and though he had his injuries, he was relieving everybody's anxiety. Miss Berta was concerned about AJ going back to school. Weeks passed, the injuries on AJ's face healed, Miss Berta took it upon herself to convince Henrietta that AJ should return to school, to complete his graduation requirements. Henrietta did not want to hear of it. She wanted her son to recover from his injuries.

AJ wanted to go back to school, he agreed with Miss Berta, but kept his thoughts to himself. It was the first time in years, his mother grew concerned for AJ's wellbeing, he appreciated it. He was not about to get into a confrontation with her, if it was going to ruin their bonding.

Miss Berta stepped in to ensure that AJ wanted to go back to school, to pursue the requirements for graduation. AJ's college acceptances would be in jeopardy if he did not complete the school's requirements. There were constant arguments over the subject. Miss Berta realized she was getting nowhere and came to the realization that it was up to AJ, to confront his mother, because it was not her responsibility.

Once Miss Berta convinced AJ, that it was his personal decision to go back to school. Henrietta was shocked at his request. Nevertheless, she was fully convinced that he needed to go back to school. AJ attended school with members of the basketball team at West Brook High School, who were very supportive.

Henrietta appreciated the fact that she was becoming a true mother, which was a new experience for her. She worked hard all of the time. She became a caring mother, one who made dinner for him each night, who asked him about school. AJ was no longer an employee at Starr Restaurant, because his relationship with his mother improved.

20

THE HAPPIEST ENDING: GRADUATION

The room was crowded and packed with graduates from West Brook High School. Parents assembled in their seats behind the graduates, smiling. Roland Tim's dad was yelling, "That's my boy! Going to UCLA to play ball!"

Roland Tim just smiled and waved. His mother, a slim woman, was also cheering for him. Other parents were clapping. As soon as Principal Hawk made her appearance, the crowd became quiet. Principal Hawk approached the stand. AJ came gliding in, to take the *"Reserved for the Valedictorian"* seat.

"As you can see, I'm not the only one running late, our valedictorian just made it," Principal Hawk announced at the podium. The crowd snickered with laughter. AJ smiled, although Principal Hawk embarrassed him. He was so nervous, he looked back at his mother, who applauded and smiled at him. Lucas was nowhere to be found.

Principal Hawk continued to welcome parents, students, and the faculty. Everyone else applauded enthusiastically. "Ladies and gentlemen, it is with great enthusiasm that I congratulate the members of our senior class, who have worked very hard to get to this point. We are very proud of them." She continued, as the audience clapped enthusiastically.

AJ took the stand at the podium. "Welcome, class! It's been a wild year, I'm sure all of you know what I'm talking about!" AJ said. The graduates applauded and laughed. The hall echoed with noise. When the crowd settled down in their seats, silence swept the room. AJ continued his speech;

he acknowledged the parents, students, and Miss Berta for supporting him throughout his journey.

"I would like to thank the parents for supporting us. You should give yourselves a pat on the back. Getting us to this point has not been an easy task. Teachers, you were there as our support system. We thank you." AJ declared.

AJ continued to speak. Twenty minutes later, his speech came to a conclusion. Principal Hawk read out the names of the graduates, while she handed out the diplomas. Miss Berta's face lit up when each member of her class was called to collect their high school diploma. It brought tears to her eyes; it was a long road to get each student into college or trade school. Miss Berta believed each student was going to be prosperous, and there was nothing that could convince her otherwise.

Later that day, each of the students rushed to Miss Berta's side, to thank her for her support. It brought tears into everyone's eyes; it was an emotional moment for everyone.

Years had passed, since Benjamin left Henrietta and AJ. He was taking a break from music for a while. He found out through an old friend where Henrietta was living. Without an invitation, Benjamin and other guests were headed to AJ's graduation party. Benjamin approached the front door to AJ's graduation party, held at their home. He crept behind Henrietta to surprise her. Tapping Henrietta on the shoulder, she could not believe her eyes. Benjamin changed. His style consisted of a brown zipped blazer. He carried his instrument everywhere. Gasping, it took Henrietta a good ten seconds for any words to come out of her mouth.

"What are you doing here?" Henrietta inquired. Benjamin was shocked to see her. He smiled to ease the tension. "How have you been?" He asked.

Henrietta stuttered, barely able to speak. "I'm doing very well, my son is graduating. I have no complaints."

Benjamin stared at Henrietta and smiled again. Miss Berta sat by Henrietta's side. She attended the graduation to support AJ and Henrietta. "What brings you here?" Henrietta asked.

Benjamin fidgeted with his fingers, out of nervousness. "You look good, Henrietta," he replied.

"Thank you. How's your music going?" Henrietta asked.

"It's going pretty well. We've decided to take a break from touring around Africa and Europe," Benjamin responded.

Suddenly, Miss Berta looked at Benjamin with disappointment. She decided not to interfere in Henrietta and Benjamin's conversation. It took her a few moments to come to the realization that Miss Berta had been at her side the entire time. "Oh, this is Miss Berta, one of the reasons for your son's success." Henrietta said.

Benjamin felt embarrassed at Henrietta's statement. "How dare you leave me to raise a young child on my own?" Henrietta addressed Benjamin. She had the opportunity to express all the pent up emotions she had for Benjamin, since the day he left without a word.

Benjamin listened, but did not respond to the accusation.

"Keep it quiet, both of you. You both are being selfish! This isn't about either of you. This is a special day for AJ. You should be celebrating his success," Miss Berta reprimanded. Henrietta and Benjamin did not say another word.

The graduation party for AJ was a small gathering. Benjamin received his invitation months ago prior to the occasion. He stood at the corner by the punch bowl. Henrietta kept glancing toward Benjamin, who kept staring at her.

"What do you think?" Henrietta asked, approaching Miss Berta.

"What do you mean?" Henrietta replied. "You miss him, I know you do, but this man left you with a baby to raise by yourself," Miss Berta said.

"AJ does have a right to see his father," Henrietta insisted.

"I agreed, just be careful," Miss Berta warned.

AJ appeared at the front door, holding hands with Rebecca. He escorted Rebecca to meet his mother. He pushed past Benjamin, but was unaware of who he was. "Mother, I would like you to meet Rebecca." He introduced.

"Hi, how do you do?" Rebecca announced.

"Hello dear. I hope you don't mind, but I need to speak to my son about something important," Henrietta said. Rebecca shook her hand and walked away. "I have some important news for you," Henrietta whispered.

"Can't it wait, Mother? I really want you to meet Rebecca," AJ responded.

"Your father's here," Henrietta announced proudly.

Gasping with shock, AJ took a step back. "What is he doing here?" Miss Berta overheard the conversation, and immediately came to AJ's side. "He wanted to be here, to support you." She said, as she placed her arms around AJ to comfort him.

"I am fine without him. Where is he? Why is he here?" AJ asked anxiously. Benjamin had been inching towards them, and overheard the conversation. He walked toward AJ, while carrying his saxophone. He swung it out the way, AJ smiled. "Hello son," he greeted in a proud tone. Once Benjamin spoke, the crowd at the party fell silent, curious to see AJ reunite with his father. "I don't know what to say to you," AJ said to his dad.

"I wanted to congratulate you on this special day," he replied.

"Where have you been?" AJ demanded.

Benjamin was reluctant to respond, fearing that AJ would berate him for being an irresponsible father. "Son, let's go for a walk outside." He escorted AJ outside, while the entire room stared at them.

"I haven't seen you in years," AJ accused.

"I know this is a big surprise," Benjamin responded.

"It is," AJ replied sternly.

Benjamin began to tear up, as did AJ. Both fell silent as their emotions reached their limit. They both gave one another one strong, firm, grizzly bear hug. "I've missed you son," Benjamin professed.

"I've missed you dad," AJ responded. Staring out of the window, Henrietta's tears fell down her face, as she witnessed the scene.

Miss Berta was amazed at the father and son reunion. "What just happened?" Miss Berta inquired out of curiosity.

"I can't explain it, but it was a treasured moment for our family," Henrietta announced. Miss Berta made her way toward Benjamin and AJ, who were back inside the house. Benjamin looked up at Miss Berta.

"Hi, how do you do?" Miss Berta asked Benjamin humbly, as she approached him.

"Dad, this is Miss Berta, my mentor," AJ informed.

Benjamin put out his hand to shake Miss Berta's hand. "Hi, how do you do?" Benjamin added. "I'm well, thank you. I hear you're partially responsible for my son's success." He continued.

"Definitely not, AJ put in the work. I simply gave a helping hand." Miss Berta replied.

"Thank you," Benjamin answered.

"It's good to see you here supporting your son," Miss Berta said. "Indeed, Miss Berta," Benjamin replied.

"It's good to see you here," AJ interupted.

"Good to be here. Congratulations, son," Benjamin announced, while he shook AJ's hands.

Miss Berta approached Henrietta, while she was talking to a guest at the party. Miss Berta interrupted, while she handed her three full trunks of clothes. "I want you to have these clothes. They are last spring's collection, but they are still in style." Henrietta said, as she hugged Miss Berta, who was astonished.

"Thank you, my dear," Henrietta replied.

The following day, Benjamin invited Miss Berta, Henrietta, and AJ out to dinner. Too fearful to ask Henrietta directly, Benjamin spoke to Miss Berta privately. His goal was to convince Henrietta, AJ, and Miss Berta to accept his dinner invitation.

Later that day, Henrietta got off her bus and reached home. Miss Berta waited for her outside. "Miss Berta, how are you, my dear? What brings you to our door?" inquired Henrietta. Miss Berta had a change of heart for Benjamin, as she watched him try to make up for his past mistakes. He talked to his son for a long time while Miss Berta couldn't help but notice how glad AJ was for his father showing up to his graduation party. He laughed at all the jokes his father made. Henrietta was showing signs of gratitude that he had the decency to show up. Miss Berta could not restrain her excitement. "Benjamin wants to take all of us out to celebrate." She explained.

Henrietta smiled with a puzzled look. "Did he say when?" She asked.

"He's coming," Miss Berta replied. Henrietta could not get over his invitation. When AJ arrived home, she presented the idea to him.

"I think it's a great idea. Would you like to go out to dinner with your father?" Henrietta asked AJ.

"Yes Mother, I would. He has some interesting stories to share," AJ responded. Miss Berta abruptly interrupted. "So, what is the final decision?"

Henrietta said, as she turned to face AJ and Miss Berta, who looked at each other for confirmation. "We will attend," Henrietta replied.

It was a cozy, small restaurant called McFadden, located on the water. Henrietta wore a simple ruffled yellow-and-white dress that reached her ankles. It radiated against the dim lights of the restaurant. Miss Berta wore a loose shirt that hung from the shoulder, and a long black skirt, which reached her ankles.

Benjamin was already seated at the table, which was set for four, and finely decorated with silver cutlery. Opening his arms with warmth, he gave AJ a manly hug. He also hugged Henrietta and Miss Berta, as they sat down in their seats. Henrietta sat next to Benjamin. Miss Berta sat next to AJ, who was dressed in slacks and a collared shirt.

"Thank you all for joining me. I thought I would be rejected," Benjamin announced to everyone at the table.

"You deserve to be rejected!" Henrietta said smugly. Both Miss Berta and AJ laughed amongst themselves.

"Well, is everyone ready to order?" Benjamin asked, when a waiter approached. Benjamin asked everyone to proceed, while Henrietta insisted that Miss Berta order first.

"I'll have the salmon with tartar sauce, and mashed potatoes," Miss Berta announced.

"And what would you like to drink, miss?" The waiter inquired.

"Lemonade, please." He replied. Henrietta raised her hand to give the next order. "Son, what would you like to have?" She asked AJ.

"I'll have the Mandarin chicken and rice," AJ replied.

"I'll have the Caesar salad," Henrietta instructed the waiter, who wrote the order down on his notepad.

Benjamin smiled, as Henrietta continued to ignore him. "I'll have a steak and mashed potatoes," Benjamin notified the waiter.

"Sure thing, sir." AJ replied.

"How have you been, son?" Benjamin asked AJ, after the waiter left.

"I'm fine, please do tell us of your travels," AJ insisted. Henrietta looked intently at Benjamin.

"I survived as a musician. We were broke at first, but started playing at low-paying restaurants throughout Germany and France. We spent time in

Africa, to have our music reach worldwide status. We were rejected many times. Sometimes restaurant managers never paid us. The band and I realized that money would come eventually. In France, girls snuck into our hotel rooms. In Germany, women wanted to marry us, and teach us about their culture. In Africa, woman cooked food for us, to give to us after our show. We didn't know these women; all we did was perform for them. Now, the men in these countries wanted to hunt us down for stealing their women's affections. Regardless, spreading our music was the most important goal of all." Benjamin confided. Henrietta was amazed. Benjamin smiled after he closed the story.

"Awesome!" AJ announced, he was impressed by his father's travels.

"What else would you like to know?" Benjamin inquired, when the waiter brought the orders to the table.

"Benjamin, it is a pleasant story," Miss Berta announced.

"Thank you, Miss London," Benjamin said.

"I thought it was interesting," Henrietta agreed, making her presence known. She was aware that AJ was old enough to hear the tale.

"It's awfully kind to hear your stories. Thank you, Henrietta."

Henrietta turned away shyly.

"I heard you moved on, proud of you," Benjamin persisted. His mother was proud of him. She hinted to AJ, that she was going to give him a plane ticket to go Europe over the summer. She used up her savings to pay for it. The trip was organized and set up for AJ. Henrietta, AJ and Miss Berta had dinner one last time before AJ was to go to Europe.

The threesome lingered over dinner. AJ, Henrietta, and Miss Berta were seated at the table, telling each other jokes, laughing together, until Henrietta burst into tears. Miss Berta couldn't contain herself from crying. Henrietta got the airline ticket out of her handbag and handed it to AJ, who couldn't believe his eyes. He was going to Switzerland for a summer internship to study engineering and architecture. He was accepted into the program, but thought it was impossible for him to go, because he didn't have the money. His mother proved him wrong; she ended up paying for the entire trip. Miss Berta wanted to take care of the expense, but his mother insisted otherwise. AJ gave Miss Berta and his mother a hug, as each of them tried to restrain the tears in their eyes.

It was a week before AJ went to Europe; he used this time to spend with friends and Benjamin. Benjamin and AJ spent times together at Central Park, discussing AJ's future. Benjamin invited AJ to stay with him, once he came back from the trip.

The day of the trip approached, and it became difficult. It was the last time he would see his friends and family.

The Johnson case was officially complete. Miss Berta went back to work for *Miss Berta and the Family Magazine*. The release of the new issue approached. She wanted this issue to be bigger than any issue she had done. She worked night and day, discussing with her staff how to fit AJ and Henrietta life's story in the second issue of *Miss Berta and the Family Magazine*. She promised AJ she would keep in touch, and that moving on was a necessity.

Back at the office, she prepped files and informed the company that the Johnson case became a success. She got an entire class of seniors to become successful in their endeavors. While, Miss Berta had been gone, Leticia took over *Miss Berta and the Family Magazine*. The magazine stayed afloat, while Leticia sent out photographers and assistants to visit schools, to get interviews to cover gossip, relationship drama, fashion, and issues with parents. Although many teenagers and young adults continued to buy the magazine, it did not achieve sold-out status until Miss Berta returned.

Newspaper articles circled the city with stories pertaining to AJ's life as a teenager from a low-income bracket, concerning his internship to Geneva, Switzerland. It featured his goals of wanting to attend Boston University for architecture and design. One newspaper headline displayed:

Teenager emerged from the sewer: Going to Geneva, Switzerland for the summer, and then Boston University to study Architecture and Design.

Other newspaper headlines displayed:

Lady in Red Hat, Miss Berta London, big time ex–fashion editor helps teenage boy go to college.

The newspapers had a field day. *Miss Berta and the Family Magazine* reached top of the charts, alongside mainstream magazines. It was a challenge to control the press. Miss Berta was flocked by photographers and journalists, as she had been during the *Eloquent Fashion Magazine* era. Summer was approaching and AJ was asked to be on live television with his mother. This event took place a week prior to AJ's trip to Geneva.

A journalist named Kenny Latham for *Morning New York* called Henrietta and AJ the following day. Henrietta was in the living room on the couch relaxing, and browsing cable channels. AJ was in the kitchen making peanut butter and jelly sandwiches. The phone rang and AJ immediately picked it up.

"Hello, this is AJ. May I help you?" AJ replied.

"AJ, this is Kenny Latham from *Morning New York*. We would like to invite you and your mother to our television network, to be interviewed live."

"Who is on the line dear?" Henrietta called from the living room.

While, holding the telephone, AJ shouted, "Mom, it's for you!" Henrietta got up from the couch to get the telephone from AJ. "Hello, this is Henrietta."

"Henrietta, this is Kenny Latham from *Morning New York*. I would like to invite you and AJ to the set to do a live interview." Kenny Latham admitted. Henrietta accepted. "All right, we will do it." She replied.

"Great, come by the set tomorrow." Kenny Latham asked humbly.

The next day, AJ and Henrietta took a cab to the studio on Fifty-Eighth Street in Manhattan. Henrietta pushed the outside buzzer, stating who they were and they were both allowed in. Upon entry, a woman with short, ruffled hair gave them clipboards and backstage passes. "Here, these are some of the questions that will be asked. Go over them." The lady replied. AJ looked at her nametag, which read "Elisabeth."

Henrietta and AJ saw Kenny Latham, a handsome, coiffed man with black hair and a slim figure, getting prepped on the set of *Morning New York*. Elisabeth approached them, and quickly prepped AJ's and Henrietta's hair.

"All right, you're good to go on set, go," Elisabeth replied. She slightly pushed them toward the set. Kenny Latham quickly shook both their hands. "I'm Kenny Latham, please sit." He introduced himself. The three camera people were finishing the setup of their cameras, while the executive producer yelled: "In five, four, three, two, one." The entire set was silent, as Kenny Latham introduced the show. "Welcome to *Morning New York*. This is Kenny Latham reporting to you live in the biggest hub of Manhattan. Today we have two special guests, Henrietta and AJ Johnson, to share with us their story with Miss Berta London, the ex-fashion editor, and the executive producer for *Miss Berta and the Family Magazine*. We would like to talk to you, Henrietta and AJ, about your new life and how Miss Berta London helped you?" Kenny Latham continued.

"She was patient with us, she believed in us." Henrietta replied.

"What about you AJ? Did Miss Berta believe in you?" Kenny Latham asked.

"Her loyalty is irreplaceable. She has been loyal to my mother and I." AJ responded.

"Well, how did she help you and your mother?" Kenny Latham asked.

"She was dedicated to making sure my dreams came true. I wanted to study abroad, and she helped me find an internship and fill out the application. She also helped me with my Scholastic Aptitude Test."

"She became part of our family," Henrietta intervened to agree, whilst on the set.

"There you have it folks. We are now our moving on to our news segment." Kenny Latham addresses. As the segment ended, Henrietta and AJ could not believe they were just on live television discussing their personal lives.

Days later, Henrietta moved to a new place of residency one she was able to afford. The new house she bought was bigger and in a better district. There was no crime and the area was peaceful. AJ went abroad to do his summer internship, while Henrietta's income tripled, with Miss Berta's help. She had a new job as head nurse in Wilk's Hospital. She thanked Miss Berta for helping her get the new job, as head nurse. Benjamin and Henrietta stayed friends. Benjamin always came to visit her at her new home; to make sure things were going well for AJ.

AJ remained friends with his basketball buddies from Westbrook High School; he wrote them letters, even though they insisted he get a cell phone. Roland Tim and the other boys gave AJ their addresses to the colleges they were going to attend, so he could meet up with them whenever the opportunity presented itself.

21

MISS BERTA AND LETICIA PREPARE FOR GENEVA, SWITZERLAND

A month later, Leticia Benet arranged to travel to Geneva, Switzerland with Miss Berta. Their bags were packed, while they waited in Miss Berta's black SUV. Her driver started the car and drove off. Miss Berta and Leticia were fully dressed, complete with hats and gloves, which had a Parisian flare.

Leticia and Miss Berta were at the office, printing out their flight itineraries, while she approached Miss Berta with a portfolio.

"We are ready for Europe," Leticia announced with high anticipation.

"I guess this is your first time traveling to Europe?" Miss Berta questioned with a smile.

"It is in fact," Leticia confirmed. Her outfit for Geneva was a dark green blazer, worn over a sheer white blouse. She had on black slacks to accompany the entire outfit. She also wore a dark green beret. Miss Berta's patience began to wear thin.

"We are ready, Miss Berta. The car is ready with all of our things packed," Leticia said.

Miss Berta and Leticia exited the building. Outside the building, crowds of teenagers and children screamed with excitement when they saw Miss Berta and Leticia. Miss Berta walked through the crowd of people, and began taking selfies with her fans. She also signed some autographs before she and Leticia got into the car. They waved to the children, while they drove through the city, passing skyscrapers.

The taxi pulled up at JFK International Airport. The driver got out and unloaded their luggage. The airport was crowded with people trying to get to their next location.

"Leticia, I thought you hired an escort for us during this trip," Miss Berta said.

"I must have forgotten," Leticia admitted.

"Fine, make sure to get the bags on the flight Leticia."

Leticia walked up to the man in charge of handling the bags.

"May I help you, miss?" The man inquired.

"Yes, we need help with our bags," Leticia requested while Miss Berta was signing autographs. "I saw you an interview on *Morning New York*," people stated as they approached her. She watched the man get their bags onto the cart. They both followed the man with the bags into the airport. At the ticket booth, an agent greeted Leticia and Miss Berta.

"Welcome ladies, may I see your flight itineraries?" The agent addressed.

Leticia handed the ticket itineraries to the ticket agent.

"Thank you." He replied.

The ticket agent printed two boarding passes and gave them to Leticia while the man placed their luggage onto the luggage belt. Leticia gave him a tip of five dollars.

"What time does our flight leave Leticia?" Miss Berta inquired, feeling impatient with the crowd of youngsters who surrounded them.

"I booked us on the 9:00 p.m. flight, so we should arrive tomorrow at 8:00 a.m.," Leticia answered.

Miss Berta exploded; her temper was triggered because of the crowds of people taking photographs of them, as they were going through the security check. A security officer approached them.

"Ladies, is everything okay?" The officer questioned them.

"We are fine, sir, we are just anxious about the crowds," Miss Berta admitted to the security guard. To her surprise, his eyes began to widen.

"Is everything all right, sir?" Leticia asked the officer, who continued to stare at Miss Berta in shock. He shook Miss Berta's hand. "My wife and children are big fans of yours." He said, he gave Miss Berta a big hug, as the crowd of people continued to snap photos. Miss Berta took a picture with the officer, as he walked away to restrain the crowds.

"All right Leticia, let's make our way to the gate. We should be boarding soon." Miss Berta announced.

Leticia and Miss Berta placed their carry-onto baggage on the luggage belt and one by one. They walked through the metal detectors. At Gate 34 B, they saw two ticket agents waiting for them. Upon their arrival at the gate, Leticia immediately took out their boarding passes, and handed them to the ticket agents. Both agents were dressed in navy-blue dresses that came up to the knees.

"You both may board the airplane," the agent announced, as she gave them back their tickets. Miss Berta and Leticia walked down the passageway, which led them onto the aircraft.

Two flight attendants: a man and woman named Ted Williams and Beth Rica, respectively greeted them, as they boarded the plane. "Good evening, ladies." The flight attendants greeted. They smiled and made their way to their seats. Leticia sat in her seat at the rear of plane. She placed her carry-on luggage in the overhead bins and sat down. Miss Berta got comfortable in her seat in front of Leticia. The private jet was expansive, with an immense amount of space. The flight attendants approached them, as they buckled their seats.

"May we get you something to drink?" The flight attendants asked.

"Grapefruit juice," Miss Berta requested.

"Water," Leticia added.

It wasn't long after their drink orders arrived, the captain made an announcement.

"Good evening, Miss Berta and Miss Benet. My name is Spencer Hendrix and I'll be your captain for this evening. Currently, the time is 9:45 p.m., our final destination is Paris, where you will connect to your next flight to Geneva, Switzerland. Thank you for flying with us. We are ready for takeoff. Flight attendants, prepare for takeoff." Captain Spencer addressed.

The plane picked up off the ground, and the aircraft was up in the air. Miss Berta occupied her time by browsing through various fashion magazines. Leticia, on the other hand, was crunched in a ball, sleeping in a seat that transformed into a bed. The food cart made its way to serve dinner. One of the flight attendants interrupted Miss Berta.

"Miss London, we have your salmon dinner ready." She said. Beth, the flight attendant handed Miss Berta her dinner, while Ted, the other flight attendant was in the process of waking up Leticia.

"Is everything all right? What do I need to do know?" Leticia inquired.

"Nothing miss, I have your dinner ready for you." Replied Ted, while he gave Leticia her dinner order. It wasn't long after that both Leticia and Miss Berta handed back their trays and were ready to fall asleep.

A few hours later, Miss Berta was up bright and early, having her breakfast, which consisted of oatmeal and orange juice. Leticia opted for a bowl of fruit instead. In the meantime, the captain was making a morning announcement.

"Good morning ladies. We have arrived in France, please be prepared for landing. Do not forget to buckle up your seatbelts. The weather in France is currently eighty-two degrees." Captain Spencer addresses.

Miss Berta and Leticia fastened their seatbelts, as the plane was in landing mode. The plane landed on the tarmac of Charles de Gaulle Airport, both Miss Berta and Leticia gathered their carry-on items and exited the aircraft, bidding the flight attendants a farewell. They hurried to their next gate, to board the next flight to Geneva, fearful that they would miss their connecting flight. During their connecting flight, Miss Berta was flocked by a crowd of people taking photographs. Leticia become worried. "Miss Berta, what do we do?" Leticia asked.

"Let's just make it to the next gate," Miss Berta made clear as they were getting through the crowd of people.

"Madame!" The crowd of people kept shoving past one another, to get a glimpse of Miss Berta, as she continued to make her way through the airport.

"We are gate 12C," Leticia reminded her, as they approached the gate and were ready to board Swiss Air. The flight attendants accepted their boarding passes, and they boarded the airline. As they fastened their seatbelts and got comfortable, the airplane took off in the air. The flight to Geneva was three hours from France. On the aircraft, Miss Berta and Leticia discussed their plan for Geneva.

"The goal is to find a new theme for the upcoming season for *Miss Berta and the Family Magazine*," Miss Berta said to Leticia.

"Absolutely," Leticia agreed.

22

AJ'S SUMMER INTERNSHIP IN GENEVA

AJ and his fellow interns arrived in Geneva for their two-week summer program. Altogether, there were six interns on this trip. Tate was eighteen, and she and her boyfriend Olivier, were in attendance. They met on last year's study-abroad program.

It was AJ's first time going abroad, and he was studying for a period of two weeks. Tate and Olivier arrived. AJ noticed them holding hands in the lobby of the *Hotel Century Geneva*. The hotel had a beautiful view of the countryside. It was the most beautiful view AJ had ever witnessed. Olivier saw AJ with his luggage and approached him.

"Hallo, my name is Olivier. Are you here for the one-week internship program?" Olivier asked. AJ nodded his head in agreement.

"Yes I am," He responded.

"Oh, let me introduce you to my girlfriend. This is Tate Mackie."

Olivier announced, as Tate shook AJ's hand.

"Nice to meet you both," AJ said.

"Well, it looks like we are the only ones here. What is your name? Where are you from?" Olivier asked.

"AJ is my name, and I'm from Brooklyn, New York." He replied.

Olivier and Tate smiled.

"We have always wanted to go to New York for a romantic getaway," Tate interrupted.

"Yes, but we have to save our money for that," Olivier replied.

Three more people arrived at the lobby of the hotel. Henry Cleiver arrived with his large number of bags. He noticed Olivier and approached him.

"Oh, what do we have here?" Henry asked, as he looked at Tate, Olivier, and AJ in a distasteful manner. "So you still think you are better than I am, do you?" He asked the group.

"I don't think, I know." Olivier snickered, while AJ could not restrain his laughter.

"Oh, that's funny to you, is it?" Henry said, as he shoved AJ.

"Hey, what's your deal man?" AJ belted.

Two of the counselors arrived, a man named Nathan, and a woman called Ruth, who interrupted the commotion.

"That's enough! Not again you two, last year was the same drama."

Nathan said, as he scowled at Henry and Olivier. Olivier shook his head to agree, while Henry walked away to calm his frustrations. The other interns arrived moments later, were identical twins. Their names were Gabriella and Claire. Gabriella and Henry were in a relationship. AJ and Claire were the only single individuals in the group.

"All right everyone, gather around," Ruth called out, while Nathan began to read everyone's name aloud for roll call.

"Olivier," Nathan announced, while Olivier raised his hand.

"AJ," Nathan announced, while he raised his hand.

"Gabriella and Claire," Nathan declared, as he continued to do roll call. Gabriella raised her arm. "Claire and I are present," Gabriella declared.

"Tate and Henry." Nathan said, as they both raised their hands and smiled. "Present." They both called out together.

"Great, now that we are all here, I would like to give everyone an orientation packet." Nathan announced, while he began handing out thick envelopes, as he read the rules and regulations aloud.

"No going out past curfew, which is ten o'clock," he said. "Girls and boys are to sleep in separate rooms. It is now one o'clock in the afternoon. You can go to your assigned rooms. I'm sure each of you would like to do some sightseeing. Make sure to be back in the lobby at three o'clock, so I can account for those who wish to sightsee," Ruth said, while the entire group went to their assigned rooms. Gabriella, Claire, and Tate were together in one suite; each suite overlooked Lac Léman, also known as the Lac de Genève. The girl's suite was across the hall from the boys' suite. The first thing AJ did when he entered his suite, was make a call to his mother. He made it a brief call. However, it was an international one. AJ told her about his safe arrival.

"Mother, I'm doing fabulous. This place has fantastic scenery and landscape," AJ said to Henrietta.

"Have you made any new friends?" She asked.

"Oh yes, I did. Tate and Olivier. They were the first people I met upon my arrival. There's this kid named Henry who looks like trouble. Other than that, this place is amazing." AJ confessed.

"That's fantastic, my son. I am very proud of you," Henrietta admitted, smiling on the other line.

"So how is Miss Berta doing? What is she up to these days?" She asked. AJ continued to question his mother.

"She's back working at *Miss Berta and The Family Magazine*. She will join me and the rest of the interns in Geneva, but I'm not sure of the exact time." AJ dialogued. Just then, AJ heard Olivier and Tate talk amongst them. They were waiting for him to finish his conversation.

"Dude, want to come sightseeing with us?" Olivier asked. AJ nodded his head, and agreed to come along. He finished the conversation with his mother, and joined Olivier and the other group of interns, to go sightsee.

As AJ, Olivier, and Tate walked to the elevator, Claire ran behind them.

"Hey, wait for me," She cried, while they all entered the elevator.

"Where's Henry?" AJ asked.

"Henry and the beloved Gabriella decided to stay. Hopefully, they are on their best behavior. Ruth and Nathan did say that any rule breaking would have someone sent home immediately. I hope for their sakes they behave for the remainder of the trip," Claire said, as the four of them exited elevator on the nineteenth floor. They walked down the hallway and approached room 1902. Olivier knocked on the door three times. The group stood looking at one another while waiting for Nathan or Ruth, who shared a room. Nathan finally opened the door in his robe.

"What is it? I have to finish coiffing my hair!" Nathan said in a rushed fashion. "Sorry to bother you Nathan, but can we now wonder around the city for a little bit?" Tate asked.

"Fine, just be back by eight o'clock tonight." Nathan said, as he closed the door. The group rushed down the hallway, in excitement towards the elevator and exited the hotel.

The group walked along the sidewalk to a very large market area. The vendors were selling fresh cheese, milk, olives, and freshly baked bread right out of oven. Finally, they spotted a saw a small café named Clara, an intimate place with dim lighting. They decided to sit for a while, to unwind and get to know one another. Tate and Olivier ordered green tea to share. AJ and Claire were talking quietly amongst themselves.

"So you're from New York City?" Claire asked AJ.

"Yes I am." He replied.

"Awesome. I always wanted to go," Claire admitted.

"Maybe you will get the chance to go one day," AJ said.

"I sure hope so." Claire responded. AJ was curious about everyone, he was on a quest to make friends.

"What is the situation with your sister Gabriella? Why is she with that guy? He doesn't treat her very nice," AJ said to Claire, as she shivered in fear.

"Are you talking about Henry?" Claire responded, as AJ nodded his head in agreement. "Henry and Gabriella have been together for a very long time. Matter of fact, they've been together for at least four years," Claire added.

"Olivier, where are you from?" AJ asked.

"I want to make a big impression on my college applications. But, I am from France," he responded.

"Cool, this is my first time meeting people from a diverse background. Tate, what about you?" AJ asked.

"I needed to add a spectacular internship experience, to send to my college," Tate responded.

"Good to know." AJ replied.

"Hey, you two, it's getting late," Olivier announced to AJ and Claire. They stood up and left café Clara. Everyone got up and walked down the quiet street to the hotel, and each of the interns returned to their respective rooms.

The next morning, the interns gathered in the lobby with Ruth and Nathan, where they were briefed on the plan for the day.

"Good morning everyone, today we will be visiting Saint Pierre Cathedral and other tourist sites in the city," Ruth announced. The group made their way toward the Saint Pierre Cathedral. The stone building seemed secluded, but it drew their attention. Nathan gathered everyone in front of the building.

"Okay, gather around everyone." He announced.

As the group fell silent, Ruth and Nathan escorted everyone into the building. Ruth began to discuss the building's history.

"Saint Pierre Cathedral is a reformed Protestant church, built during the twelfth century with eclectic styles. It was best known as the adopted home of John Calvin," Ruth said.

"Who's John Calvin?" Henry asked, as everyone wandered throughout the building, analyzing its interior décor.

"John Calvin was responsible for the Protestant Reformation, everyone knows that," Gabriella informed Henry, who gave her an exasperated look because she knew the answer and he didn't. Ruth continued her lecture.

"Does anyone have any other questions?" Nathan asked.

Henry raised his hand. "Well, I have to use the restroom," he admitted.

"The restrooms are located throughout town, but I'm sure there's a restroom in the building," Claire said.

"Can I go? I'll find the location," Henry requested.

"I think it's best if everyone take a restroom break," Nathan interrupted. The group dispersed. Henry went along with Gabriella, while AJ and Claire went together to explore with Tate and Olivier.

"We all know that they did not go to the restrooms," Tate whispered in a joking sort of way.

"Who cares, they are both idiots." AJ laughed to himself. Claire stood next to him, while AJ poked fun at everyone. Henry and Gabriella suddenly appeared, overhearing their conversation.

"So, you're still going to give us a tough time here?" Gabriella declared in front of everyone. Gabriella and Claire did not get along with each other. Claire wasn't a big fan of Henry either. AJ decided to defend Claire.

"Dude, please tell Gabriella to back off," AJ announced.

"Make me Brooklyn boy," Henry snarled.

"Yes I live in Brooklyn, New York?" AJ answered.

"I know all about you and that mentor of yours, Miss Berta London," Henry admitted. AJ's eyes were shocked that Henry knew his private life.

"How do you know that?" Olivier intervened.

"Dude, mind your own business." Henry snickered. Henry continued to mock AJ. Meanwhile, Claire defended him.

"I agree, what on earth is your problem?" Claire challenged Henry, just as Oliver stepped in to stop the disturbance.

"That's enough, all of you!" Nathan bellowed, annoyed at the entire group for bickering. Everyone fell silent.

"Good, so let's get on with the tour. I have to teach you about different styles of architecture," Ruth said, as everyone began to exit the cathedral. The interns observed the stone building from the outside, taking pictures of all its adornments.

"As you can see my friends, it was built for the Protestant believers," Nathan interrupted. The interns stood outside the structure listening to Nathan and Ruth, who continued their lecture about the building's history.

"We are to visit architectural structures, to analyze them and get a deeper perspective. This internship is to teach you about culture and design. We will gain wide knowledge concerning these areas," Nathan continued.

The group's next destination was the Palace of Nations. Everyone stood on the premises, admiring the many flags of different countries.

"This is the original headquarters for the League of Nations. It was built in 1920 as a result of the Paris Peace Conference, which ended World War One. The League was the first international organization, whose mission was to promote world peace. It has been replaced by the United Nations. It has 193 member states. As you can you see, it is made of stone and waves a row of international flags," said Ruth, as the interns took notes, as she described the historical buildings.

The next site they embarked on was the Jet d'Eau. The interns took out their cameras, as Nathan gave them details about the structure.

"Jet d'Eau is a large fountain in Geneva, and one of the famous landmarks in the town. It was installed in 1888. Five hundred liters of water per second are jetted to an altitude of one hundred meters." Ruth said.

"Well, I think it's time for lunch. Why don't we take an hour break?" Nathan declared. The interns dispersed; Henry and Gabriella landed at an Italian restaurant called Ricardo. To their dismay, they noticed Olivier, Tate, AJ, and Claire enter the restaurant. A hostess approached Henry and Gabriella, and sat them at a table by the window. Another host sat Olivier, Tate, AJ, and Claire nearby. Claire took a paper napkin and scrunched it. She ducked her head and threw it, while it landed on Henry's head. He belted aloud.

"What is going on?" Henry said, as he stood alarmed, while Gabrielle calmed his nerves.

"They're here, and they threw paper," Gabriella informed Henry.

"Whom are you talking about?" Henry demanded.

"The other interns," Gabriella said. Henry immediately stormed over to their table in a huff of anger.

"What is the deal?" He declared.

The group continued to laugh.

"Dude, just calm down. We were just having a bit of fun. Don't take it personal Henry," AJ replied.

Henry stood silently and thought of the ridiculousness of the situation, and laughed alongside Gabriella, who followed him to their table. Each of them couldn't help but laugh at the hysterics.

"Just join us. Let's put our differences aside," Olivier announced aloud, as he invited them to their table. Henry and Gabriella nodded in agreement, and sat down with them at their table.

23

A BIG COINCIDENCE, THE WILLIAMSONS

Nick and Jessica Williamson were part of a new group of interns, who were also interning at Geneva, Switzerland. They attended the same internship program as AJ, Olivier, Henry, Tate and Gabriella and Claire, but were with different counselors, because of the differences in age. Upon their arrival, the new group of interns had also gotten permission to go sightsee the town of Geneva. Nick and Jessica decided to exempt themselves from the other group of interns. They made their way to Ricardo Restaurant. Olivier noticed them as they walked in.

"What is going on with all of these interns coming to dine at Ricardo?" Olivier said, as he noticed all interns wear badges, which were in green and gold displaying "Geneva Interns." Each intern was required to wear these badges, when they were wondering the town.

"Coincidence," Tate responded.

Nick and Jessica saw Olivier, Tate, Claire, and AJ and decided to make their acquaintance, because they dreaded the other interns in their group.

"Hello," Jessica Williamson greeted. Everyone from the group looked up at Nick and Jessica, while AJ was surprised.

"May we join you?" Nick asked with a welcoming smile. In the meantime, AJ pulled up chairs for them to sit at their table. Jessica and Nick sat down. Jessica immediately struck up a conversation with AJ, who sat across from her.

"AJ, you made it?" Jessica insisted, with enthusiasm.

"It's good to see you Jessica. How's the music going?" AJ inquired.

"Not bad," Jessica replied.

"Why don't you sing for us?" AJ insisted, while the others agreed with him.

"Yes! Go for it!" Henry and Nick shouted.

"We agree!" Tate, Gabriella, Claire, and Olivier chimed in. The room clapped with encouragement. Jessica gave in and made her way to the forefront of the restaurant.

"Hello everyone. My name is Jessica Williamson. Although I do not have my band members with me, I will sing for you." Jessica cleared her voice, and waited for everyone to get quiet. She began to sing:

> *"Do you believe in slumber? I do, I do.*
> *I believe in the good times, when it was just me and just you.*
> *Never give up on the good times.*
> *Never say goodbye.*
> *Always try to be happy.*
> *Because, it's is your lullaby."*

The audience was moved by her voice, each of them clapped and cheered for her. She simply smiled. Suddenly, a stylish woman walked into the restaurant. She wore a red beret hat, a green jacket, and brown platforms. The entire restaurant fell silent. Couples and families whispered among themselves at the sight of her. Leticia was mentioned as part of the conversation, as the restaurant hostess escorted them to the table. In the meantime, Jessica, Olivier, Tate, AJ, and Claire turned their heads. They were in awe and shocked at the sight before them. Nick and Jessica made their presence known. They approached Miss Berta and Leticia's table. Miss Berta was amazed when Jessica and Nick greeted her.

"Miss Berta, what on earth are you doing here?" Jessica inquired, shocked to see her. Miss Berta turned toward Jessica, dumbfounded.

"Oh my goodness children, where did you come from?" Miss Berta said, while hugging Jessica and Nick. AJ approached Miss Berta and tapped her on the shoulder.

"Oh my goodness, all of you are here!" Miss Berta cried.

"I finally get to meet you in person." Leticia addressed AJ, who was confused.

"Who are you?" AJ inquired curiously.

"My name is Leticia, the lady who introduced you to Miss Berta over the telephone." Leticia confessed. AJ simply shook his head. "Well, nice to meet you Leticia." He replied. Leticia responded with a smile. The waiters arrived with the food. Jessica, Nick, and AJ returned to join the rest of the group. After they sat down, Gabriella leaned forward with anticipation.

"Okay, do you personally know Miss Berta?" She asked.

"She used to be our nanny," Nick Williamson confessed.

"She helped me graduate from high school. She also helped me land this internship in Geneva." AJ told the rest of the group, while Jessica listened intently.

"She helped us bond with our parents and become much closer as a family," Jessica said.

"All of this is great, but we all should eat quickly, and get back to the counselors. They will be worried if we are late," Henry interrupted. Everyone at the table nodded in agreement, and ate their food.

Miss Berta approached the interns at their table.

"Would you all like to spend the remainder of your day, helping me choose themes for the upcoming *Miss Berta and the Family Magazine*?" Miss Berta announced.

"Absolutely!" They replied with excitement.

"Good, I received permission from all of your counselors. They wanted a day to themselves, to explore the city. However, they did give me a list of things on the itinerary, which they would like us to do." Miss Berta said.

Leticia distributed paper and pens to them, after everyone finished eating. Each of the interns used the list of activities Ruth and Nathan provided Miss Berta. Many of the topics written were sights and things they wanted to do, during their stay in Geneva.

"Where are all of you staying?" Miss Berta inquired as the interns continued to write down their ideas.

"Hotel Century Geneva," AJ responded, as he continued to draw the Lac de Genève, with each intern standing before the lake, while making silly faces.

"That is a coincidence," Miss Berta mumbled to herself.

Olivier couldn't help but overhear Miss Berta mumble under her breath. "Why do you say that?" He questioned.

"Because that is the exact hotel we are staying at," Miss Berta said to Olivier.

"Hey, what are you going to do with the information we give you?" AJ inquired as everyone handed in the ideas to Leticia.

"Well Leticia and I are going to browse the town, to get more ideas for the upcoming issue. We are going to pair the ideas you submit with ours." Miss Berta explained, as everyone looked up at her with anticipation and excitement. Meanwhile, Gabriella stood up, to remove herself from Henry's grasp.

"Well, I know for a fact that I am going on this escapade to shop, instead of participate in the activities Nathan and Rush wish for us to accomplish," Gabriella announced.

"I am going, I am not about to let her have all the fun," Claire admitted.

"But Miss Berta, she doesn't even like fashion," Gabriella said to Miss Berta.

"How would you know?" Claire demanded out of anger.

"You couldn't possibly be serious," Gabriella added.

"Girls, that is quite enough! All of you are welcome. We could use as much diversity as possible," Miss Berta responded.

"Well, I'm not going back to the uninteresting historical tour with Nathan and Anna," Tate confessed.

"Well I better go too," Olivier decided.

"Me too," Henry announced.

"Well of course, we're all going." Olivier said, as he looked toward AJ.

"Very well. It's a pleasure to have all of you make a contribution to the magazine." Miss Berta acknowledged everyone, while Leticia gathered the paperwork from the interns. The interns gathered their belongings. Miss Berta and Leticia set out to tour Geneva. The sun was shining. Miss Berta wore her fancy sunglasses, while Leticia carried a large bag.

"All right everyone, gather around. All you have to do is tell Leticia, where you would like to go, and she will photograph it. Many of these ideas will be featured in the upcoming magazine. Each of you will be featured also." Miss Berta said, as she escorted them to the Musée d'Art et d'Histoire.

"This museum was built in 1851. Its fine art section has paintings from the middle-ages-to-the-twentieth century. They have a wide range of works from Italian, Dutch, French, English and Swiss art." She escorted the interns outside the museum, while they chatted amongst themselves. Leticia gathered everyone around, ensuring that everyone was accounted for.

"Right, you may all walk along Avenue 49 Blanc for some personal exploration time. Be back in an hour, do not go beyond this street." Miss Berta warned, as the interns scattered. Olivier and Henry had their eye on a nearby chocolate shop.

"Guys, Henry and I are going in here." Olivier announced to the others, as Henry followed him inside a chocolate shop called Choco. Inside the shop were pipes of chocolate intertwined throughout the store.

"It's an actual chocolate factory." Henry said.

"Dude, this is incredible." Olivier replied back. They both observed the atmosphere, while AJ, Tate, Claire and Gabriella joined them in the store.

"What are you all doing here? Find your own hobbies." Olivier said to the others annoyingly.

"So, why are you guys in here?" AJ asked out of curiosity, Henry and Olivier put their differences aside, to complete the assignment they had planned for the summer.

"Henry and I are doing a documentary over the summer, to enter into the Cannes film festival," Olivier replied egotistically.

"On chocolate? Who cares about chocolate?" Tate interrupted sarcastically, while the others laughed at her response.

"Do you know that chocolate is big business? Not to mention, Olivier and I are going to be chocolatiers one day. We are going to go into business together after college," Henry replied defensively. Meanwhile, Gabriella, Claire and AJ tasted the chocolate samples, which were on display.

"I can't blame them. This is a delicacy." Gabriella said, with a mouth full of chocolate.

"I agree." AJ replied, as he tasted a few chocolates. Tate was ashamed for being disapproving of Henry and Olivier's future goal.

"Dude, never mind them. We should do a chocolate tasting," Olivier said to Henry. Meanwhile, an elderly, short man approached them.

"Bonjour," the man said.

"Bonjour," they replied.

"May I assist you with a chocolate tasting?" The man asked with a smile.

"No thanks, we would like the owner to conduct the tasting. We are looking for information on how to become chocolatiers." Henry said beguilingly. The man simply smiled.

"I am the owner of Choco. My name is Jean Pierre. I have owned this shop for sixty years." The elderly man replied.

Henry and Olivier were in complete awe.

"Sir, we apologize," Henry replied.

"Yes, please excuse us," Olivier echoed.

"Well, let's get on with it. Now I was a big kid, obsessed with chocolate. I worked for a man, who owned a chocolate store, which became my influence to want to get into chocolate making. I went to school right here in Geneva. Not to exaggerate, but Geneva is known for its chocolate delicatessens. I sell most of my chocolates in ski resorts like Crans Montana and Verbier in the Swiss Alps. Those are the largest ski resorts in Switzerland, well-known tourist destinations." Jean Pierre said, as he walked them through a row of chocolates.

"You are more than welcome to taste some, I've mixed rich cocoa and vanilla over here. In the next aisle, I've decided to mix berries and nuts grown locally in Geneva. Boys, the secret to chocolate making is simple, less sugar and more cocoa." Jean Pierre said.

"Sir, may we take a selfie of you?" Olivier asked as he held up his camera.

"A selfie? What is that, son?" Jean Pierre questioned.

"A picture sir," Olivier replied.

"Oh yes, of course you can." Jean Pierre said, as he gave a big smile. Suddenly, Miss Berta walked into the shop.

"Goodness, there you are," Miss Berta interrupted. "What is going on here?" She asked.

"Chocolate tasting and a brief history lesson," Jean Pierre replied.

"Sir, we would like to feature you in *Miss Berta London and the Family Magazine*."

"Yes, it is a family magazine. It would be great for you and the shop." Miss Berta insisted.

"All right, then I am convinced." Jean Pierre agreed. Miss Berta handed Jean Pierre consent form to sign. He read the material and signed it, so he could be featured in the upcoming issue of *Miss Berta and the Family Magazine*. Miss Berta saw the chocolate tasting section of the shop, and tasted a few chocolates.

"Sir, these are scrumptious. Are you the chocolatier for this shop?" Miss Berta asked.

"I most certainly am." Jean Pierre replied.

"Well in that case, we will take a dozen of those chocolates on the tasting displays." Miss Berta said, as she began to take out her wallet.

"Absolutely not, I would like to give you the chocolates free of charge." Jean Pierre smiled. Olivier and Henry took a few pictures of Jean Pierre wrapping the chocolates, while Miss Berta took some pictures of Henry and Olivier standing before Jean Pierre.

"We can never thank you enough for your hospitality sir." Olivier admitted, as both he and Henry shook his hand.

"Here take my card." Jean Pierre said, as he handed Miss Berta, Henry, and Olivier each a card. Meanwhile, Jessica and Nick were in a guitar store. Nick was taking an interest in music, like Jessica. As they both were playing around with the guitars on display, Nick approached Jessica.

"Jessica, can I be part of your band?" Nick inquired.

"You've been harassing me for years on that topic. I will let you, but you have to learn how to play." Jessica replied.

"Well, you could teach me." Nick said.

"Of course," Jessica replied, while Miss Berta walked in on them.

"What are you two doing? I am so happy to encounter you two. I have so many fond memories of you." Miss Berta admitted.

"We've missed you too." They said, as they gave her a big hug. Nick was showing Miss Berta some tunes, while Jessica sang along.

Tate and Gabriella were looking for clothing stores, trying different styles of vintage pieces. They were the last group Miss Berta had visited. This gave Leticia some time to herself, to go souvenir shopping while Miss Berta made rounds to check on everyone.

"Tate and Gabriella, clothes and clothes make the world go round." Miss Berta said, interrupting the girls and their shopping.

"Miss Berta, just the woman we need to see. What do you think?" Tate asked, as she showed Miss Berta a pile of clothes.

"Miss Berta, Tate and I are having trouble choosing," Gabriella confessed, while Miss Berta simply smiled.

"Ladies, the rule to fashion is to make a statement." Miss Berta confessed.

"What do you mean?" Gabriella asked inquisitively.

"Choose clothes that you like and that are unique. Be the anomaly," Miss Berta responded. The girls began to analyze the clothes in the hands.

"Thank you Miss Berta," Tate and Gabriella replied simultaneously.

"All right girls, I am going to go check on AJ." Miss Berta said as she exited the store.

It didn't take Miss Berta long to find AJ. He was settled comfortably on a sidewalk. He sat with a notebook and pen writing as he watched the people walk by. Miss Berta approached him and sat next to him, exhausted.

"Hey Miss Berta," AJ said, as he continued to write notes.

"AJ, what are you writing?" Miss Berta asked.

"My entire trip to Geneva so far. This place has been incredible. Geneva is rich in culture and history. I am writing about the chocolate shop, the historical tourist destinations, everything I have learned so far about this country. This country has taken my breath away." AJ replied.

Miss Berta listened intently. She began to watch the time on her watch, and noticed the other interns approach her. She stood up from the bench, while Leticia was the last to approach the entire group.

"I wish I could show you more, but I must be going." Miss Berta said, before leaving Leticia to take over. The interns were not happy that she decided to abruptly leave. She walked away, leaving Leticia to handle the rambunctious lot of teenagers. Meanwhile, she made her way back to Hotel Century Geneva. She was fatigued from the eventful day. As she entered the lobby, the front desk agent greeted her. "Welcome back Miss Berta." He greeted.

"Thank you, Thomas," she replied as he held up two envelopes.

"These letters arrived through the express pickup." He said, while he handed them to Miss Berta. She took them and headed toward the elevator, and pushed the fourth floor button. She approached the door to her hotel suite, which had MISS BERTA'S SUITE labeled on the front door in gold lettering. She entered and noticed various fruit baskets, and flowers in her suite; orange and white lilies were filled with some of the finest Swiss chocolates. Miss Berta sat down on a large luxurious sofa, taking off her boots to get comfortable. She opened one of the envelopes and read the letter inside.

> *Dear Ms. London,*
> *I miss seeing your face, when I deliver packages to your residence. I wish*
> *I knew if you missed me. I am in love with you. I know you probably*
> *have important things to do during your Geneva visit, but I thought that*
> *I should let you know how I feel.*
> *Sincerely,*
> *Travis. The deliveryman.*

As Miss Berta read the letter, she could not restrain a smile. She folded the letter and placed it back into the envelope. She read the second letter she received from Henrietta, it read:

> *Dear Miss Berta,*
> *I miss him tremendously. You too, are also on the list of the ones that*
> *I miss. I know the upcoming feature for Miss Berta and the Family*
> *Magazine will make you into a bigger star than the old Eloquent*
> *Fashion Magazine.*
> *Good Luck, Henrietta.*

Meanwhile, Nathan and Ruth finished eating their pasta dishes at a restaurant near Lac de Genève. They paid for their meal, and began to worry about the whereabouts of the interns.

"Calm down Ruth. Stressing over the situation is not going to help us find them sooner." Nathan said, as he grew tired of her impatience.

"All right, where should we start to look for them? Should we notify the police that they are missing? Should we notify their parents?" Ruth rambled.

"We are going to look for them. If we do not know of their whereabouts by morning, we have to notify the authorities in this town. We also have no

choice but to contact their parents. It is the responsible way to handle it."
Nathan responded, anxiously. Ruth and Nathan were on an active search
throughout the city. Nathan asked people in French if they saw a group of
youngsters wonder by the Jet d'Eau or the Musee d'Art et Histoire, but they
did not have much luck. Ruth called each intern's cell phone, but did not
receive any responses. She checked Ricardo restaurant, hoping they visited,
but they were not there.

The interns were running Leticia ragged. She could not rest at all. They
were demanding about whic photographs should be featured in the upcoming magazine. Leticia lugged her luminous camera around the city, taking
snapshots of the Lac de Genève. On one side of the lake, swans floated
along, calm and peaceful.

"Did you take a shot of the swans?" Jessica asked.

"I did. Thank you, Jessica," Leticia replied. Jessica insisted that Leticia
take a snapshot of the interns being silly.

"I agree, that is a great idea," Leticia concurred.

"All right everyone, be as silly as you possibly can," Leticia announced.
The interns stood before Lac de Genève with zeal. Henry boosted Gabriella
onto the rail, while AJ put his hand on his hips and smiled. Claire jumped
on AJ's back, while he continued to stand with hands on his hips. Tate
jumped into Olivier's arms. They looked like two newlyweds. Jessica and
Nick both faced opposite directions with their arms crossed. They each
grouped together to take the picture. Leticia smiled at the intern's hysteri-
cal antics.

The following day, the news revealed that counselors Ruth and Nathan
reported the interns as missing, because they had not returned from their
lunch break with Leticia and Miss Berta the day before. Nathan and Ruth
were on the prowl along with the authorities, searching for the young adults.
The news of the missing young adults began to spread throughout Geneva.
Leticia and Miss Berta were considered the culprits. The local media iden-
tified them as kidnappers. Miss Berta could not understand the faces that
scrutinized her, as she walked down the street to the nearest café, which
was located one block from the hotel. She ordered her usual chocolate croissant with hot chocolate. She had not been informed about the interns going
missing.

A slim waiter approached her. "Is there anything else I can get for you madam?" He asked, as he placed the chocolate croissant, and hot chocolate before her.

"That will be all, thank you." Miss Berta replied.

Meanwhile, the waiter named Paul raised his eyebrow. He recognized Miss Berta during the live local news report, and immediately picked up the phone in the café, to dial the Hotel Century Geneva's telephone number. Thomas, the front desk agent picked up the telephone.

"Hotel Century Geneva. This is Thomas, how may I help you?" He answered.

"Yes, my name is Paul and I'm calling from Jean Claude café, located a block away from your hotel. I've spotted Miss Berta. You can notify the counselors Nathan and Ruth." Paul, the waiter hung up the phone.

Thomas immediately telephoned Nathan.

"Hello, it's Nathan," He answered.

"Hello sir, it's Thomas from downstairs at the front desk. I've received whereabouts concerning the location of this lady, who may know where the interns are," Thomas informed him. The phone rang in Ruth's room, and she immediately answered.

"Hello?" She greeted.

"It's Nathan, get dressed. We have a lead concerning the whereabouts of the interns. Meet me in the lobby." He said, while he hung up. Shortly after, Ruth was downstairs wearing jeans, a white blouse, and a brown cardigan, waiting for Nathan. He approached her with determination.

"What is it? Where can we find this person who will link us to the interns?" Ruth questioned.

"Just follow me Nathan," He responded, while he led Ruth out of the hotel and down the street toward the Jean Claude café. They entered, and Nathan approached Miss Berta, who was taking a bite out of her chocolate croissant.

"We are here to ask you if you have seen our interns," Nathan interrupted, as Ruth stood silently.

"Oh goodness." Miss Berta said belligerently.

"Yes we had no choice, but to proclaim the children missing. They are under our watch," Ruth contested. Miss Berta listened intently, and continued to drink her hot chocolate. She finally put down her mug of hot chocolate and began to address Nathan and Ruth.

"Goodness, I completely forgot to mention to you that the interns preferred to join me on a tour of the city, till early morning. They arrived late last night in their hotel suites. I just received the message from my assistant, a few moments ago. She states this is on live television. How ridiculous, that the news forgot to report that they arrived at two o'clock back in their suites. My assistant Leticia was their escort around the city. They are compiling ideas for my upcoming magazine feature. My assistant had your permissions in writing, that you gave your consents." Miss Berta admitted.

"I'm sorry, but we did not allow that. Your assistant did not finalize the decision with us. We agreed the interns would remain under our supervision," Ruth contested in fury.

"Their parents were worried. We had no choice but to notify them concerning what happened," Nathan admitted, while Miss Berta smiled.

"I can assure you, they are in good care! There is no need for the theatrics!" Miss Berta announced. Nathan and Ruth began to feel assured, but were worried.

"Can we at least have your contact information? We need to be aware of the interns' whereabouts," Nathan said. Miss Berta shook her head in agreement. "Absolutely, I understand." She replied. Miss Berta gave Nathan and Ruth their own individualized business cards. Upon finishing her hot chocolate and croissant, Miss Berta paid and left Jean Claude café.

Leticia was at the other end of the city with the interns, brainstorming ideas for the upcoming magazine release.

"All right everyone, any more ideas?" Leticia asked the interns. Gabriella raised her hand to respond. "We should interview a sales representative from Tara." She said.

The rest of the interns agreed. Tara was a high fashion store in the city for both men and women.

"I guess I'll do menswear," Henry added.

"How about us boys represent the menswear department?"

AJ suggested.

"Great idea, Gabriella, let's make our way over there now."

Leticia said, while the interns walked over the street toward the Tara building clothing store. They were greeted by one of the Tara sales representatives.

"Hello. May I help you?" The stylish lady addressed them, as they entered Tara.

"May I speak with your manager?" Leticia asked. The sales representative disappeared, and returned with a man dressed in a suit.

"Hello, may I help you? My name is Claude, and I am the manager here at Tara." Claude shook Leticia's hand and looked mesmerized. "I know you!"

Leticia said, with a puzzled look on her face. "How is that possible?" She asked.

"You're Miss Berta's famous assistant, who wouldn't know you?" Leticia smiled at Claude's remark. "Thank you sir. We would like to interview you and your employees about Tara. Our interview will be featured in the release of our new issue of *Miss Berta and the Family Magazine*. The interns will be featured, promoting Tara." Miss Berta confessed, while Claude smiled.

"Please, I must get the permissions from the employees and customers first." Claude said, as he walked around getting the necessary signatures for the contract proposed to him by Miss Berta. The last signature was signed and the interview began.

Gabriella wasted no time asking questions. Leticia took out her camera and began to take snapshots. Henry began to take snapshots. Henry interviewed the sales representatives, while AJ and Claire interviewed the customers, while they shopped in the store.

The shop began to get crowded and rowdy over the lack of customer service, because of the interview sessions, which took place. Nathan and Ruth were among the customers. It was a coincidence that they were in the same shop, unaware of what was taking place. AJ recognized them and tapped Claire on the shoulder.

"Nathan and Ruth are here," AJ announced to Claire. Henry, Olivier, Tate, and Gabriella also noticed Nathan and Ruth in the store.

"Olivier, Nathan and Ruth are here." Tate whispered to Olivier, who was interviewing a customer, concerning the reasons why Tara was the number one place to shop. Gabriella and Henry continued to question the customers.

Leticia decided to stop taking snapshots, as Nathan and Ruth slowly approached her, while Claude was helping a customer.

"Hello Leticia. We apologize, but we would like you to be aware that we are the counselors for these interns," Nathan addressed Leticia directly.

Leticia was overwhelmed as Nathan and Ruth confronted her.

"I work for Miss Berta and she let me know that you both are aware of their whereabouts." Leticia replied, concerned.

"We did speak with her earlier regarding this arrangement." Ruth announced. Leticia refrained from responding. She simply nodded her head.

The interns approached Leticia concerning the incident. As the counselors walked away, Leticia was taking snapshots of the building. She did her best to forget the encounter of the counselors.

"At least we can all continue working on ideas for the new magazine," Olivier declared before the group.

"I agree." Tate continued, while Henry and Gabriella held each other's hands. AJ and Claire could not help, but smile at the situation.

Claude approached her. "Well, it is about time to wrap things up." He said. Leticia nodded her head in agreement, and began to put away her camera equipment. The interns followed her toward the exit. She led them past a high school, students chattered among themselves in the schoolyard. The interns stood outside the gates of the high school, watching students sitting on the grass.

"We should take some great pictures of us together." Olivier announced to Leticia.

"Absolutely, I agree." Henry concurred, while Leticia took out her camera to snap photographs of the interns, while they stood before the school gate.

"Wow, this is great." Gabriella declared.

"Would you stop jumping around and stand still. She's taking a photo of all of us." Henry said as AJ, Claire, Olivier, and Gabriella stood in front of the school, taking snapshots. Leticia took photographs of the interns, while they posed for the camera. Her last photograph was of the interns smiling at one another.

"All right, time to get back to the hotel," Leticia announced, while the interns began to moan at the idea.

"There is so much more to see," AJ said.

"Now is not the time to complain. Our time here in Geneva is very short." Leticia announced, while the clan discussed their individual family backgrounds on the walk back. AJ agreed he would not have been on this internship in Geneva, had it not been for Miss Berta. All the interns were impressed that Miss Berta was acquainted with AJ and his family.

Back at the Hotel Century Geneva, Ruth and Nathan awaited Nick and Jessica's return. Nick and Jessica ran into Leticia in the lobby.

"We just want to thank you for accepting us as stowaways." Said Jessica, as they made their way toward the lobby's elevator. They got into the elevator together. When they reached their floor, Nathan and Ruth went to their suites. Jessica and Nick continued onto a higher floor.

The other interns found Miss Berta seated on one of the couches in the lobby, sipping coffee. She smiled as she saw all the interns standing alongside Leticia.

"Miss Berta, how are you?" AJ called as the other interns followed his lead.

"Jessica and Nick, made their way upstairs," Miss Berta announced in a lively tone to Leticia, who was across the room.

"You are absolutely correct, Miss Berta," Leticia replied.

"How was their tour of Geneva?" Nathan asked AJ, taking a seat.

"I am enjoying it. I am learning about the historical sites. I cannot wait to share the news with my mother," AJ admitted to Miss Berta and Nathan, who simply smiled at his excitement and enthusiasm.

"Agreed." Henry admitted, as he placed his arm around AJ in a brotherly fashion.

"Wow, you two are best friends now? Things have changed during the course of this internship." Gabriella said, as Claire nodded her head in agreement.

"Well interns, Leticia, and I are going to use all your great ideas from the Geneva trip for the upcoming issue of *Miss Berta and the Family Magazine*." Miss Berta said. The children applauded with excitement, when Miss Berta made the announcement. Nathan and Ruth simply looked at each other, wondering if their presence was going to be acknowledged.

"Well, we enjoyed the free time roaming around the town in search of the interns." Nathan snickered sarcastically, as Ruth placed her arms around him in a friendly manner.

"You definitely made this trip one to remember," Ruth concurred.

Miss Berta stood up to make her final announcement. "Well, it is getting late, but out of curiosity, Nathan and Ruth, what did you do this whole entire trip?" Miss Berta asked with anticipation.

"Well, besides looking for our interns, we decided to make the best use of the time," Ruth admitted, crossing her arms together.

"Do elaborate on your statement," Leticia interrupted.

"Well, we did a lot of shopping, sightseeing, discovering different restaurants; the usual tourist things." Nathan replied.

"Great, not to be rude, but it is getting late, and we all need to pack and get ready for our flights." Miss Berta addressed the group, as she walked away from the scene.

"She is absolutely right. Get your things packed for your return flights home," Ruth announced, as she and Nathan instructed the students regarding their departure the following day.

"All right everyone, upstairs to your rooms," Nathan instructed. The interns made their way toward the elevator and headed upstairs. Leticia decided to take one of the adjacent elevators to her hotel floor. Nathan and Ruth were the last to leave the lobby. Everyone returned to his or her respective hotel suites.

Nick returned to his roommate, Glen, a young fellow around the same age as he was. He was silently folding his clothes into his suitcase. To Nick's dismay, he was in a state of shock to see him enter.

"Where have you been mate?" Glen addressed Nick.

"I was with another set of interns on this trip. Also, I am going to be featured in the upcoming *Miss Berta and the Family Magazine*," Nick told Glen, who was filled with immense excitement and enthusiasm. Glen's eyes widened with disbelief.

"Are you serious, Nick? Miss Berta, the famous fashion icon?" Glen exclaimed without restraint.

"Of course, I'm serious. Jessica and I regrouped with other interns and ran into Miss Berta at this café, and she offered to have us and a few others be featured in her next magazine release." Nick said, while he could not refrain from excitement, as he went on and on about his adventure around Geneva.

"Did anyone wonder where I was?" Nick asked, very anxious to hear Glen's response.

"Well, the entire group went out looking for you and Jessica, but I did have a feeling you were okay. I did cover for you. We all have to pack our things, because parents were worried when the rest of you went missing." Glen admitted.

"I guess I should alert the counselors." Nick sighed as Glen nodded his head in agreement. Nick exited the room and knocked on one of the hotel rooms down the hall, which marked room 404.

"Coming." A loud voice responded, while the door flew open. A middle-aged man with ruffled hair was extremely shocked to see Nick.

"Nick! Where have you been? We've sent out people to look for you!" Winston cried. Winston was Nick and Jessica's butler.

"Well thank you Winston. I am doing quite well, if I do say so myself," Nick announced confidently.

"Do tell, where have you been?" Winston demanded.

"Well Jessica and I found another group of interns and we decided to tour the city of Geneva along with them." Nick hesitated.

"I feel you are leaving out something," Winston said.

"Well, you won't believe who we ran into during our tour of the entire city," Nick confessed.

"Who?" Winston asked, unable to contain his curiosity.

"Miss Berta London," Nick replied. Winston's eyes widened with shock.

"Well, I'm sure your reputation will improve around here because of it. Pack up your things and get ready for tomorrow. You, Jessica and I have a flight to catch. It is my duty to make sure you arrive home safely to your parents." Winston reminded him and left.

Nick nodded his head in agreement, and walked back down to his hotel room. Glen, his roommate packed his bags, and was in the process of brushing his teeth. Nick simply began folding clothes, and placing them into his brown suitcase. He took his time folding shirts and pants neatly, then placed his sneakers on the side of his suitcase. When Nick finished packing, he crawled into his single bed. Glen was asleep in his pajamas in the other single bed, snoring. In another room down the hall, Gabriella and Claire slept until the alarm located between their beds went off. It rang and rang until Claire slowly lifted the covers over her head.

"Gabriella, please turn it off!" Claire yelled angrily.

"Why do I always have to turn it off?" Gabriella announced groggily. She slowly got out of her bed and turned the alarm sound button off. Groggily, she shook Claire out of bed jokingly.

"Claire, wake up. It's eight o'clock, time to catch our flight home." Gabriella said. Claire jumped out of bed and hurried to the bathroom. She closed the door behind her, as Gabriella rushed around the hotel room to place smaller items into her bags. Claire exited the bathroom fully dressed. Gabriella immediately rushed into the bathroom to get ready. She could hear Tate knocking on the door.

"Gabriella, I'll be downstairs in the lobby waiting for you. I'm ready." Tate announced, as she grabbed her luggage. Her dark hair was in a messy bun. She exited the hotel room with her luggage trailing behind her. Meanwhile AJ, Henry, and Olivier were waking up. Henry got up and made his way to the bathroom. Olivier brushed his teeth. AJ turned the television on for the weather and news updates, while they waited for Henry to get out of the shower. Henry came out of the bathroom, fully dressed and ready to go downstairs.

"Dudes! Henry said, while AJ and Olivier ran toward the bathroom. AJ slammed the bathroom door on Olivier.

"Sorry, I got here first," AJ called. Henry exited the room along with his luggage. Meanwhile, Olivier scrambled around the room to pack the remainder of his belongings. It wasn't long afterwards; AJ came out of the bathroom fully dressed. He immediately grabbed his luggage and exited. Olivier rushed into the restroom.

In the lobby, AJ was talking to Claire, while Gabriella sat next to Henry. Nathan and Ruth were in the lobby, reading off flight information for each intern.

"Gabriella?" Ruth announced.

"Present." Gabriella raised her hand.

"Claire?" Ruth continued to announce.

Claire immediately raised her hand and refrained from talking to AJ, who was too busy playing around with the nearby floral decorations. "Present." She said aloud as she raised her hand

"Good, the girls are ready," Ruth told Nathan. Nathan began to read off his list of interns, ensuring that everyone was present.

"Where is Olivier?" Nathan asked, immediately recognizing that Olivier was missing.

"He's still upstairs getting ready," AJ informed him.

"Thank you AJ," Nathan responded. Out of the blue, Olivier appeared, dragging his luggage behind him.

"Present." Olivier announced.

"Good, we were beginning to panic." Nathan replied.

"No need for that type of drama," Olivier joked. Nathan chuckled. Nathan continued to do roll call, marking everyone's presence. "Henry and AJ." He announced.

Henry and AJ raised their hands. "Present." They replied.

"All right everyone, time to start for home." The interns gathered their luggage and began to board the airport shuttle, which had been waiting for them outside the lobby.

24

MISS BERTA AND THE FAMILY MAGAZINE: INTERNS TAKE GENEVA, SWITZERLAND

Heather sat next to Romero before a crowd of fifty people in Central Park.

"We need to go back and support our previous boss," Romero announced. Miss Berta's old team from *Eloquent Fashion Magazine* gathered on the grass, applauding Romero. Heather stood beside Romero, crossing her arms. "We need to leave our current careers and join *Miss Berta and the Family Magazine*." Romero began to whisper in Heather's ear, "The plan is to surprise her." He whispered.

"How?" Heather asked in a concerned fashion. "Anna has done her research, she is propelled to go back and join Miss Berta. Let's face it, we could do so much for children and mix fashion in the midst of it all. We have been stuck in the adult fashion world, and I don't know about you, but I am sick of the problems and the stress it creates. Think of how good children and young adult fashion could be for us, professionally. Miss Berta has changed. These young adults and children have affected her in positive ways. No adult could ever bring about such change in her spirit," Romero attested.

Heather listened to the plan to rejoin Miss Berta and her new magazine. She sat quietly and patiently, as the people in the crowd spoke among themselves. She enjoyed the breezy wind and sunlight. She watched dog owners, and watched fellow mothers with their children. She looked upon her son's face. Her son stood in his overalls, watching the other children run with cones of ice cream in their hands.

"I'm sorry, Romero, but I cannot go through with this." Heather decided and picked up a picnic basket from the ground with her belongings: her blue purse, her polka-dot wedges, and her son, who clapped for Romero, while he smiled.

"I'm sorry Romero, I cannot continue with this proposal. Do you recall how I was mistreated?" Heather said.

Romero looked sternly from Heather to her son. Heather's son looked up at him, wide-eyed, and continued to chew on the candy in his mouth.

"Why would you call me here if you knew how I felt about her?" Heather asked.

Heather's son tugged at her long dress.

"Quiet, Mommy's talking." She said, as her son acted out his frustrations toward Romero, who was responsible for taking his mother's attention away from him.

"Heather, there is no other person I know as strong as you. There is no other person whom I trust as much. Yes, back in those times we were under scrutiny," Romero admitted.

"She treated us terribly," Heather interrupted.

"I agree with you," Romero replied, Heather crossed her arms and pouted. Meanwhile Romero placed his hand around her shoulder. "We can do this. Think of your son, he could part of the magazine. If you don't do anything else, please think about it." He said. Heather nodded her head and held her son's hand. He was in awe by the games the other children played in the park. Heather and her son left Central Park, as Romero continued to inspire the rest of the crowd from *Eloquent Fashion Magazine* to go back to work for *Miss Berta and the Family Magazine*.

"We have to go back and surprise her, let her know that her old staff are one loyal bunch. We do not abandon each other. This isn't about fashion. This is about something so much more than that. This is about the connection each of us had with one another. We created *Eloquent Fashion Magazine*. It is our responsibility to join *Miss Berta and the Family Magazine*, and take the magazine to a new level." Romero implied.

Back at *Miss Berta and the Family Magazine* headquarters, Miss Berta and Leticia were in Miss Berta's large, extravagant office, looking at the final copy of the new upcoming issue.

"I approve, but I need an extra day to think about it," Miss Berta added.

Leticia gave her a questioning look, "I understand Miss Berta, but why the hesitancy?" Leticia asked.

"Ah Romero, I missed his style of photography. Words cannot describe the appreciation that I had for his art." Miss Berta confessed.

"I miss him too." Leticia confessed. Suddenly, there was a tap at the door.

"Hello, I couldn't help but overhear the conversation." Heather said, as she entered Miss Berta's office with Romero. As they entered, they took everyone by surprise. Miss Berta turned to face them.

"What do you think of the sample issue Heather?" Miss Berta inquired. The final piece of the magazine represented the interns, touring the city of Geneva. The photographs featured an interview written by Olivier and Henry. Alongside the written interview was also a picture of them and Jean Pierre, the chocolatier from *"Choco"*. The written interview was described as pleasurable and exciting. Tate and Gabriella wrote a piece for the fashion section of the magazine. There were photographs of them in the clothing store Tara, alongside them was Miss Berta, who gave them advice on fashion, and quotes she mentioned. There were excerpts from AJ's journal, giving his thoughts about the Jet d'Eau, Mussée des Arts, the Cathedral, and the town of Geneva and all its history. AJ's photo was featured alongside his travel writings. Last, but not least, Jessica and Nick wrote a piece on guitars that were made in Geneva, Switzerland. They compared and contrasted the guitars that Jessica owned, detailing the materials and the sound of the guitars from the shop they visited in Geneva. Leticia and Miss Berta were featured in the magazine. Heather looked at the magazine Miss Berta handed her. She was immensely impressed by the color design and the concept of the new issue. There was a small passport-size photograph of Miss Berta on the left-hand side, detailing her goals for the magazine and her biography. She wore a bright red French beret, with bright red lipstick on her lips. She had on a mixed brown-and-red overcoat. Miss Berta's career timeline was at the bottom of the biography.

The interns' photograph from the Geneva visit was displayed on the front cover. AJ and Tate smiled, while Henry had his arms crossed, with Gabriella standing next to him with a grin.

"Miss Berta, it is perfection. Leticia and I, and the rest of the crew know we made a successful issue." Romero declared. "Have faith in us, your entire crew has come back to you, because we aren't quitters. We want to be with you for the down part of the industry, but most important, for the upside." The entire crew nodded their heads in agreement, while Romero intervened.

Miss Berta gave her approval to release the magazine. The extravagant image of the interns standing before the Jet d'Eau, along the articles outlining each intern's experience, featured in the new issue.

New York City residents from all sorts of demographics became interested in the feature of *Miss Berta and the Family Magazine: Interns Take Geneva Switzerland* and her Geneva interns. Magazine readership spread like wildfire. Its reputation circled from Geneva to neighboring European countries like Spain, Portugal, Africa and Italy. The magazine also reached Asian countries like Japan and China, and was a huge hit in the United States. The new magazine issue drew attention from all walks of life. The photography and computer graphics from Romero captured the architecture of the 180's Swiss buildings. The success of the magazine drew a large tourist crowd to Geneva. The interns, who focused on fashion, wrote their articles from their perspectives, which gave Miss Berta worldwide appeal.

Miss Berta grew more popular because of her unique ideas, concerning the family dynamic she witnessed from the two distinct families, the Williamsons and the Johnsons. Although the Geneva trip was over for Jessica, Nick, AJ, Olivier, Gabriella, Tate, and Henry, each of them became beloved throughout Geneva. The magazine was the beginning of a successful comeback for Miss Berta.

A week had gone by since AJ's return from the trip. Henrietta loved listening to the details of his internship. It wasn't long afterward. AJ found himself in his room, packing to get ready for college in Boston. He telephoned Miss Berta to keep her updated about this new endeavor in his life.

Travis was now Miss Berta's official boyfriend, they traveled to the Bahamas. On a night out, they strolled hand in hand along the beach, laughing together. Travis slowly dropped to one knee in the sand, and asked for Miss Berta's hand in marriage. Miss Berta was in awe; she could not believe what was happening. She was frightened at the question, but Travis was direct and clear. She cried tears of joy, and Travis was relieved at her response, because her answer was yes.

Miss Berta alerted Henrietta with the good news, and was delighted.

The telephone conversations with AJ and his mother went well. "I am doing extremely well mother, don't worry about me, please tell Miss Berta that I said that," AJ persisted. Nevertheless, Henrietta and Miss Berta were pleased to hear the good news from AJ's first year, as a freshman in college.

Gustave Vero appeared in the lobby of *Miss Berta and the Family Magazine*. The place was decorated with flowers, and sounds of classical music played in the background. Miss Berta's assistant, Leticia approached Gustave. Gustave handed her a letter, then placed his black cowboy hat on his head and exited the building.

Knocking on the door three times, Leticia waited. "You may enter," Miss Berta announced. She was in the process of writing a response to a young boy, who wanted to have the opportunity to meet her, to discuss ideas for incorporating cartoon characters into the magazine. Leticia entered with the sealed envelope from Gustave. She carried it in a tray toward Miss Berta. Looking up at Leticia wide-eyed, "What is it?" She inquired.

"A letter," Leticia replied.

"Yes, from who?" Miss Berta said, with a displeased look of fear and anger in her eyes.

"It's from Gustave Vero," Leticia responded.

"What does he have to say to me?" Miss Berta announced harshly, while she pointed in the direction of the door, "Get rid of it, please." Miss Berta said.

"Miss Berta, you might want to consider reading this letter, maybe he has thrown in the towel, perhaps offering an apology," Leticia suggested.

"Read it to me," Miss Berta asked. Leticia opened the top of the envelope, which was written in Gustave's cursive writing. Leticia began reading the letter:

Madame Berta London,

S'il vous plait, pardonnez-moi.

It is to constant regret, that I humble myself and apologize to you with sincerity. I want to offer an apology, and refrain from destroying your reputation as a fashion mogul, who has tremendously influenced not only the thriving metropolis of New York City, and the world. The world has looked to you for inspiration and guidance. It wasn't my place to interfere. Please do note that I was only doing what was required of me as an employed journalist. I am aware of the shutdown of Eloquent Fashion Magazine and believe me when I tell you, that I do blame myself partially for twisting the words from your old staff a long time ago. Please excuse my forward question, but please allow me to ask you to meet with me at Memoriam Restaurant, known for having diverse types of food from all over the globe. No worries, it is all on my tab. What do you say? I would like to reiterate the fact, that I am extremely sorry for my ludicrous, improper, deceitful behavior toward you. I only want to mend the dissension we had between one another, professionally.

Sincerely,

Gustave Vero

P.S. I love the direction you are taking Miss Berta and the Family Magazine.

Reading the last words from the letter, Leticia folded the letter meekly. She looked at Miss Berta, who could not contain her composure, as she sat at her desk. She began to sob.

"Miss Berta!" Leticia cried.

"It has nothing to do with you Leticia. That's the jerk who was responsible for undermining my whole career at *Eloquent Fashion Magazine*," Miss Berta replied.

"I know, I wonder what brought him to do this?" Leticia said.

"Guilt, my dear," Miss Berta replied.

"So what is your decision?" Leticia looked intently at Miss Berta.

"I will go meet him," Miss Berta decided.

Leticia was in disbelief at her response.

"Leticia, take out a pen and respond on my behalf," Miss Berta directed.

"Yes Miss Berta. What do you want me to write?" Leticia replied.

Miss Berta dictated her response, while Leticia wrote down the response:

> *Monsieur Gustave,*
>
> *This is a confirmation, that I have received your letter. I am in complete awe, that you of all people would reduce yourself to an apology. I do admit it was quite refreshing to listen, as my assistant read to me your words of apology. To answer your question concerning the invitation, I accept. Please note, that your past actions have not been erased from my mind. Nevertheless, I am a very forgiving person, once forgiveness is earned. You picking up the tab is definitely a start toward that goal. I will need you to give me a specific date of your availability to confirm this rendezvous. Once my assistant is aware of the date and lets me know, I will be glad to confirm the date proposed.*
>
> *Signed,*
>
> *Miss Berta London*

Leticia placed down the pen and handed the letter to Miss Berta, who was reluctant to sign her signature at the bottom.

"If you need a minute, I completely understand," Leticia responded.

"I just can't believe this. What an unexpected surprise." Miss Berta said, as she picked up her ink pen, to sign her name in big cursive writing. She placed a stamp of approval. "I want this delivered, Leticia."

"I can do that," Leticia announced.

"All right, send it through high-priority express mail," Miss Berta directed.

"Yes ma'am," Leticia replied. She exited Miss Berta's office, and took a seat at her desk. Miss Berta picked up her office phone, to call Leticia.

"Leticia, I need this letter sent out as soon as possible. When does the next mail get sent out?" Miss Berta asked.

Leticia picked the telephone and called the office mailman. A man on the other line of the telephone responded in a calm, collected tone. "In the next five to ten minutes, Ms. Leticia. Someone will be up on the fifth floor to pick up the mail." He replied, on the other line.

"Thank you," Leticia replied and hung up the phone.

Miss Berta was dressed in a long navy-blue gown that covered her shoes. She had a white feather in her hair. Her limousine driver escorted her out of the car.

"Thank you sir," She said.

"Not a problem miss," the driver responded.

Gustave Vero waited at the entrance of the restaurant Memoriam, wearing a tuxedo. Crowds of elegantly dressed people were allowed to enter. The security guard at the front door asked for photo identification. There was a large European place setting for a group of ten people. The waiter, a tall slim man named Ricardo, escorted them.

Upon taking her seat, Miss Berta inquired, "Why are we seated at a ten-place table?" She asked Gustave. Gustave took Miss Berta's hand. "Well, I have a surprise for you," he announced.

"What could you, of all people, do to surprise me?" Miss Berta replied.

Gustave Vero instructed a group of ten people to enter, by a signal to the waiter. To Miss Berta's surprise, her past employees from *Eloquent Fashion Magazine* entered the dining area of the restaurant. Miss Berta gasped in shock. "What is happening?" She blurted aloud.

Romero approached Miss Berta and gave her a hug.

Heather approached her and gave her a hug.

"Now, this is definitely a shock." Miss Berta said, as she smiled. Heather smiled back at Miss Berta, while Romero looked at her for confirmation. "We would like to come back to work for you," Miss Berta's old team from *Eloquent Fashion Magazine* announced proudly.

Miss Berta fell silent, stunned. "Is this a joke?" She asked, bewildered.

"We're serious." They replied with enthusiasm

"We have decided to come back and work for you," Anna, Miss Berta's former assistant confirmed. Miss Berta smiled, in agreement to this announcement, "I accept." She replied.

Meanwhile, Lucas was on the run. He was worried the authorities would pick him up. He came to the conclusion that he should leave town. He grabbed his baggage at Central Station in Manhattan. A ticket agent approached him, as he sat down on one of the benches at the train station.

"Sir, where are you headed?" The ticket agent asked.

"I'm headed to Chicago," Lucas announced as he removed the ticket from his wallet to give to the ticket agent.

"Why Chicago?" The ticket agent asked.

"Well, to start a new and peaceful life," Lucas responded.

The ticket agent nodded in agreement. "New starts are sometimes a necessity, to fix who we are." The ticket agent replied.

"I agree sir," Lucas added.

"Cheers to you and your new beginning. Just so you are aware, sir, the train will be leaving shortly." The ticket agent instructed.

Lucas nodded his head once more, while the ticket agent walked away. He gave Lucas back his train ticket. Lucas began to break down in tears, as he reflected on his behavior. He thought about his mistreatment of AJ and Henrietta. He could not understand where this behavior surfaced. Nevertheless, he took a note card, found a blue pen, and began to write a letter to Henrietta and AJ.

> *Dear Henrietta and AJ,*
> *This is to address my unwanted presence in your lives. I have clearly made a mess of things, and all I can do at this point is to leave the state definitively. This is for the both of you to be in peace. I just feel for once in my life, I should do the right thing. I wish the both of you happiness and joy.*
> *Take care, Lucas*

The loudspeaker announced the train headed for Chicago. Lucas quickly placed a postage stamp on the envelope and put the letter inside his pocket. He boarded the train to Chicago. Several hours later, the train stopped at the Chicago train station, Lucas gathered his belongings and exited the train. He placed the envelope in the nearest blue mailbox inside the station. The letter was now in the process of being sent.

It took three days for Lucas's letter to arrive at the Johnson home. Henrietta arrived home from work and checked the mailbox. Henrietta entered the front door with a slew of mail in her arms. She immediately noticed the letter from Lucas.

"Oh no!" Henrietta belted.

"Mother, what is it?" AJ inquired; he was still on his break from college life. Henrietta dropped the letter on the floor. AJ stood up to pick up the letter from the floor.

"Mother, please sit down. You are making me nervous." He said.

Henrietta followed AJ's instruction, while he began to read the letter aloud, after he ripped open the envelope. Henrietta listened to every single word.

"Mother, it's an apology." AJ replied.

Henrietta nodded her head. "It is good news that we shall never hear of him again." Henrietta said to AJ, while he nodded his head.

"I agree Mother." He replied.

25

THE RELEASE OF THE NEW ISSUE

It was a typical rainy day in New York City. The commotion on the city streets was more intense than usual due to the weather conditions. Traffic was at a standstill. The cars beeped their horns with impatience and lack of empathy for pedestrians. Lines and lines of people flocked in crowds around the streets to purchase their copy of the new magazine.

"Come get your copy!" One of the newspaper vendors announced at the crowds. The copies sold by the millions. The fresh magazines sat on the forefront of each vendor's stall. The magazine, *Miss Berta and the Family Magazine: Interns Take Geneva, Switzerland,* was captioned in cursive with the photograph of the interns standing before the Lac de Genève. It was the photograph that was taken by Leticia, Miss Berta's humble assistant.

Police officers were maintaining traffic along the side of the streets, to ensure the flow of traffic picked up. The crowds of young people became impatient with the vendors. They wanted their copy immediately.

At the top of the *Miss Berta and the Family Magazine* headquarters, Leticia was stationed at her office desk, answering numerous incoming telephone calls.

"Greetings, Miss Berta's office. How may I be of assistance?" She replied.

The voice on one of the phone lines was Romero.

"Any good news?" Leticia inquired.

"I'll be right there," Romero responded with enthusiasm. It wasn't long, he arrived at the office to meet Leticia and Miss Berta for the updates.

"Is there anything I must know?" Leticia asked, deeply concerned.

"Well, I bought three of the copies, which I had to stand in line for. The lines are backed up, definitely a promising sign," Romero responded.

Leticia could not help herself, but smile. "That's great news." She belted.

"Well, we must wait for the boss," Romero said, as he sat himself in Miss Berta's office. The door slowly opened. Romero and Leticia headed to the doorway, to welcome her.

"Welcome back, Miss Berta, we have some *great news*!" Romero excitedly explained. Miss Berta smiled, as Romero continued to report the good news.

"The magazines are selling," Leticia announced, as Miss Berta hung her brown coat on the coat rack. She placed her suitcase on her desk.

"I anticipated the outcome from this magazine. The suspense is torture. Staying at home is unproductive. I would like to know how well the magazine is doing so far." Miss Berta admitted.

"I agree, the suspense is difficult to bear." Romero nodded his head in agreement. Leticia also agreed with his statement with a nod. Miss Berta decided to take a walk through the city, to witness the sight of her fans buy the new magazine. She was aware that she would be recognized, as the exceptional fashion icon of this present era. Leticia and Romero followed behind her.

Outside on the streets, crowds of people continued to shove and push each other. They held up traffic for pedestrians. Although the streets were vibrant with people, vendors, bookstores; many people were preoccupied with owning their copy of this magazine.

"Come get your copy!" A wide man with a mustache addressed the buyers, who approached his stall. He was thrilled to have sold all the recent copies of the new issue. The man noticed Miss Berta strolling through the city and became excited at the sight of her.

"Oh my gosh! Is it really you, walking past my vending stall?" He cried.

"It certainly is. May I ask a favor of you? I need you to play it smooth and act, as if I was never here." Miss Berta replied.

He was beside himself. Miss Berta walked along the street, passing many vendors, who were also selling the new magazine. Many pedestrians witnessed her strolling the streets of New York. She started to attract attention from the onlookers, who began to snap photographs of her from every angle. Romero indicated to people to refrain from filling the streets. The crowds were out of control. Some strange, obsessive fans began pulling Miss Berta's garments. Romero placed his arms around Miss Berta in a bear hug, to protect her from people pushing and shoving into her.

"Out of the way! Let us pass!" Romero alerted the crowd. He turned to face Miss Berta with a severe glare on his face. "I think it's time to make our way back," he said. She nodded her head to agree.

Back at the office, Miss Berta was disheveled from all of the pushing and shoving that happened outside the headquarters.

"I think I've seen enough for one day." Miss Berta said, as she took a seat at her desk. "The issue is an outstanding success, more than I ever anticipated." She added.

Leticia came in with a bottle of water and a decorated glass on a tray. She opened the water and poured it for Miss Berta.

"Thank you Leticia." She replied.

Leticia nodded her head. "I'm glad that the magazine is a big success." Leticia said to Miss Berta.

"I am pleased concerning the release of the new magazine, but I find the outcome to be surreal and unexpected," Miss Berta replied.

"I very much anticipated this outcome. I wanted you to make a comeback, and you did. We are all proud of you." Leticia admitted.

"Thank you for believing in me. I couldn't have gotten this far without all the love, and support from all of you." Miss Berta replied, while she gave Leticia and Romero a hug. She began to pack up her briefcase. She placed a copy of the new issue inside.

"Would you like to come out and celebrate? This is a special occasion. One that should be remembered," Romero suggested.

"Thank you Romero, for the kind words, but I think all of us should go home, relax, and be with our families. We could all use many days of rest. We all have been working extremely hard to accomplish this success." Miss Berta acknowledged her entire team, for their hard work.

Meanwhile, on the other side of town, AJ spent time with his mother.

"Well, you definitely have made your father and me very proud of you," Henrietta announced.

"Thanks Mom," AJ replied.

"You deserve it," Henrietta said as she gave AJ a big hug. They both smiled.

"I want to give you something." Henrietta took something from her backpack.

"Here, this is for you." She said, while she handed him a gift-wrapped package. "It's a present," she announced as AJ began unwrapping the paper. Inside was a magazine. He read the title. It read in bold: *Miss Berta and the Family Magazine: Interns Take Geneva, Switzerland.*

THE END

ABOUT THE AUTHOR

Jihan Latimer is an inspirational writer who has always had a passion for the written word. Ever since grade school, she has taken it upon herself to keep a journal at her side and write whatever she thinks, making up her own adventures. This passion she had for the written word has stuck with her throughout her life. She feels very blessed and honored to have her first novel published. She has done a great deal of traveling in her lifetime and only wishes to share those experiences with her readers. She was born in Washington, DC, but grew up around the world.